Bottom
Line

A Salt Mine Novel

Joseph Browning   Suzi Yee

Text Copyright © 2020 by Joseph Browning and Suzi Yee

Published by Expeditious Retreat Press
Cover by J Caleb Design
Edited by Elizabeth VanZwolle

For information regarding Joseph Browning and Suzi Yee's novels and to subscribe to their mailing list, see their website at https://www.joseph-browning.com

To follow them on Twitter: https://twitter.com/Joseph_Browning

To follow Joseph on Facebook: https://www.facebook.com/joseph.browning.52

To follow Suzi on Facebook: https://www.facebook.com/SuziYeeAuthor/

To follow them on MeWee: https://mewe.com/i/josephbrowning

By Joseph Browning and Suzi Yee

THE SALT MINE NOVELS
Money Hungry
Feeding Frenzy
Ground Rules
Mirror Mirror
Bottom Line
Whip Smart
Rest Assured

Chapter One

Captain Takaharu Nakagawa looked out upon the dark waters as he guided the *Hideki Maru* into position over the South Solomon Trench, thirty miles east of Santa Ana Island. He and his crew of eight—six experienced Japanese fishermen and two novice Solomon Islanders learning the trade of commercial fishing—set out shortly before sunset to make the most of the darkness. When you harvested for squid, you sailed at night.

The old but reliable diesel engine complained as its captain powered it down, and grumbled one final time even after it was technically shut off. The crew joked that it was like a mother-in-law and a lazy uncle rolled into one—it always got in the last word when you turned it off, and it took a long time to get going when you wanted it to work.

Built by Imabari Shipbuilding in the late 1980s, the *Hideki Maru* was a 150-ton vessel that had caught many different types of squid in its lengthy career, but most recently focused on firefly squid. It was now even doing diplomatic work in the process. It was one of six test ships in a six-month pilot, a collaboration between Japan and the Solomon Islands wherein the Japanese gained some fishing rights in the Islands' territory, provided they educated the locals on sustainable, relatively low-tech commercial fishing techniques. The negotiations had been long and elaborate, but such was required to strike a mutually beneficial deal. All eyes were on the pilot program ships; should they prove successful, there would be dozens more.

The crew had only worked together for three days, and admittedly, there were challenges. Teaching the greenhorns how to fish had been trying for the seasoned sailors, especially because they had to rely on English as a shared language and only one of the Japanese fishermen and one of the Solomon Islanders considered themselves proficient in that language. Communication was essentially a lot of multilingual yelling that eventually boiled down to two men speaking English—neither of which were native to it—who then dispersed the information to the others. However, they all shared the language of profit and were in high spirits after they delivered their first shipload of squid at the newly re-opened processing factory in Honiara. They had spent most of the return journey tallying up the value of their respective shares in the haul, and their initial success made all aboard look forward to the next catch.

There was methodical order to squid fishing, and once everyone on-board understood the process and their role, it simply came down to repeating the cycle until the holding tanks were full again. Speed and muscle memory would come with repetition, troubleshooting with experience. The first step was attracting the squid, which Captain Takaharu Nakagawa took care of with a flip of a switch, illuminating the massive thirty-thousand watt lights that loomed over the superstructure of the *Hideki Maru*. No one knew why squid were attracted to light, but fishermen throughout the ages had used it to draw the cephalopods to the surface in large groups.

Once the lights were on, the crew began the hour-long process of transporting the net from the main deck to the smaller inflatable boat lashed against the stern. The net was the crux of the whole operation; mainlines attached individually to the ship's winches were threaded through both the top and bottom of the net. Buoys lining the top allowed the net to hang like a mesh curtain in the water and encircle the seas around the ship. In order for the massive net to properly unfurl in the water, it had to be carefully folded like an accordion and moved that way at all times, but the long loading time didn't go to waste—it gave the squid plenty of time to gather around the light.

Once the net was in place, the ship's winch pulled the bottom of the net together, using the mainline like a drawstring and cinching it closed. Then the three crewmen in the skiff used long poles to push the buoyed top of the net under the *Hideki Maru*, freeing the large ship from its net and allowing it to pull in the catch. The haul was then deposited into water-filled tanks on the ship, keeping the squid alive while they fished until it was time to cash in another load at the processing plant. It was a simple method, repeated nearly a dozen times during an average night as the *Hideki Maru* moved along the north ridge of the South Solomon Trench.

Unfortunately, tonight was not an average night despite its familiar beginning. After he confirmed that "mother-in-law" had finished talking back, Captain Takaharu Nakagawa flooded the nearby waters with light. Two Japanese fishermen and one Islander got into the skiff and transported the net with the help of crewman on the main deck. They slowly trawled out the net behind them, encircling the *Hideki Maru* as the ship gently rocked in the small waves of the still night. A large school of squid had come to investigate the lights, unaware the ship's winch had just sealed the bottom of the net together. The three crewmen in the skiff started in with their long poles, establishing a rhythm to avoid crossed poles.

"The net's clear! Start the winch!" Tomohiro Tada called out in Japanese as he pushed the last of the floats clear of the *Hideki Maru*. As an extra measure, he banged the hook at the end of his pole against the metal side three times; sometimes it was hard to hear shouts from the small boat while at the winch controls, but the clang of the metal always came through.

The triple tap also signaled Peter Nawo to reverse the outboard motor on the skiff. He slowly trawled backward a dozen yards before killing the engine, far enough to ensure it was well clear of the net during extraction. It took the *Hideki*

Maru about fifteen minutes to pull in the big net, and the crew of the small boat took advantage of those minutes to relax. While the initial ventures were filled with uncomfortable silences, familiarity had loosened their tongues. They'd started teaching each other their languages, saying an English word they all knew and then trying to get each other to correctly pronounce the Kahua and Japanese versions. It was a good way to pass the time, and by the end of the night, inevitably a flask of whisky would get passed around. In fact, "booze" had been the first word that prompted their little game.

The men in the skiff were on "apple" when the *Hideki Maru* finally pulled the writhing mess of squid out of the water. True to their name, the stressed firefly squid flashed a cobalt blue with their bioluminescence, lighting up the mass with tiny bolts of blue lightening. Bolts of blue dripped from the bottom of the net as it rose out of the water—a few squid escaping and returning to the sea, their light fading as they descended into the darkness below. The display brought a quiet hush over the three men in the skiff, abruptly ending their language lesson. It never ceased to evoke awe in its terrible beauty. Even though they knew better, they couldn't help but feel like they were doing something wrong.

As the haul hovered over the *Hideki Maru*, the winch operator relaxed the bottom line, releasing the ton or so of squid into the watery holds in the body of the ship. The *Hideki Maru* was projected to fill their tanks and return to port thirty times in their six-month pilot, but the captain remained hopeful to exceed that, if the catch from the past few days was indicative of what was to come for the rest of their trial period.

With the catch onboard and the net empty, Nawo started up the small boat's engine and tooled to the lowered stern of the *Hideki Maru*. The two sailors with him secured the inflatable boat to the larger ship, and all three jumped out—it was all hands on deck to fold up the net for the next cycle of fishing.

As they worked the now-familiar pattern, the *Hideki Maru* suddenly yawed a full ten degrees to port, bringing the two new Solomon Island sailors to their knees as well as two of the experienced Japanese sailors. Captain Takaharu spun his chair to the bow, looking for what could have pushed the nose of the *Hideki Maru* more than ten feet, but there wasn't anything in the still water. "Everyone okay?" he called down to the deck.

The fallen sailors righted themselves with assistance from their fellows. "Everything's fine!" Tomohiro responded once he'd checked. "What happened?"

The captain's shrug went unnoticed by the men as the *Hideki Maru* twisted again to its portside, and the Japanese sailors instinctively dropped to their haunches, an instinct drilled into them early on when the ground of their homeland shook during one if its many earthquakes. Captain Takaharu looked down at the brightly lit water on the starboard side, this time seeing the wake of something's retreat without making out its actual form. Judging from the waves, one thing was certain—it was coming in for another pass. Captain Takaharu bellowed out to his men, "Brace for impact!"

Chapter Two

Scuba Dreams III, East of Cairns, Australia
7th of August, 6:05 a.m. (GMT+10)

David Emrys Wilson woke as the ambient light grew just a little brighter over the Pacific Ocean. Wiping the sleep from his eyes and rolling onto his left side, he peered through the tiny porthole facing eastward. The incipient dawn coated the underside of the lingering cloud cover in a layer of pinks and purples; they would burn away as soon as the fiery ball finally broke the horizon. Wilson watched the sunrise over the Great Barrier Reef in silent appreciation—he still had his earplugs in. Once the sun had solidly risen into the sky, the piercing shimmer off the water forced him to pull down the window cover and look away.

He pulled the foam from his ears, gingerly maneuvered out of his thin wooden bunk, and quietly climbed down the steel ladder in case his cabinmates were still asleep. Halfway down, he realized his effort was unnecessary because Matt and Francesco weren't in their bunks; they had left without waking him—a fact he chalked up more to his earplugs and being in the top of three bunks than to their stealth. Even though he was on vacation, he was still a little bothered that they'd been able to sneak out without waking him.

He'd initially been suspicious of winning an all-expenses-paid vacation from his local classical music station's pledge drive, and had eventually decided against going. After hearing him "dick around about it"—as Dot had put it— for several weeks in an uncharacteristic bout of ambivalence, the librarians used some of their prodigious abilities to confirm that it really was just the luck of the draw. Chloe had more tactfully argued that it had been more than two years since he'd taken any real time off of work, and not all good things were a convoluted plan to isolate him for an assassination attempt. So here he was, although he'd still brought his normal traveling gear; he wasn't foolish.

Wilson quickly changed out of his nightclothes and into a pair of thin, tan linen pants and a breezy black cotton long-sleeved shirt, but not before applying a thin layer of SPF 100 and double-checking that his shark-tooth choker was secure around his neck. He was always the most-dressed of all the guests aboard the *Scuba Dreams III*, but if India had taught him anything, it was to cover up against the sun. The Northwestern Australian sun wasn't something to trifle with, even if it was technically winter in the Southern Hemisphere. Normally, he wasn't a fan of sunscreen, mostly because it inevitably smelled like some sort of slightly-off coconut-slash-banana hybrid, but he wasn't going to spend the day diving without it.

The smell of fresh toast and the sounds of newly sizzling bacon greeted him as he opened the cabin door. "Finally up, I see," Francesco teased as Wilson slid into his chair at the long communal table.

"We thought you'd be out for hours," Matt added. He was sitting next to Francesco, and both of them were enjoying the first fruits of the kitchen.

"I sleep heavy on vacation," Wilson responded. "The water didn't hurt." Everyone nodded in agreement—the gentle waves they'd had last night lulled them quickly to sleep as well. Today was the last day of a three-day, two-night tour of the Great Barrier Reef; although everyone was exuberant from the experience, there was a tinge of ennui, knowing it would soon be ending.

Half of the group were new and just discovering the wonders that lurk beneath the waves, while the others were experienced divers. Wilson was solidly in the latter half; he'd been diving since he was a teenager, and most of his vacations incorporated seeing some new underwater area. He'd been to the Great Barrier Reef twice before and, given the fact that it was dying, suspected this would be his last visit. He knew the trip organizers were picking the best spots within their sailing range, but there was still a lot of white where once there was color. It was one thing to know it was happening and quite another to witness it—he didn't want to watch something so wondrous fade away into eggshell nothingness.

Once breakfast was over, he hit the water. The first time he'd stripped down to his suit, his mass of scars drew attention. Fielding the normal battery of questions, Wilson had delivered the same lie with comfortable familiarly: bear attack. It always made for a dramatic story, one that he'd told enough times that he sometimes almost believed it. It was certainly preferable to the truth; he could gladly go the rest of his days without remembering the karakura demons ripping into him in the darkness of an abandoned Japanese coal mine.

As one of the few on board with solo certification, Wilson had sole discretion on where he could roam, provided he remained within a quarter mile of the *Scuba Dreams III*. Each morning, he'd found out where the majority of the divers would be for the early dive and headed in the opposite direction. He had other reasons for solitude than his generally misanthropic nature; he was trying to charm fishes.

Surprisingly, fish charming was quite demanding; according to the Salt Mine, only a few practitioners had ever managed it. A variety of reasons were cited for its difficulty, but the general consensus was that human magic had an inherent air-based component that was rather antithetical to the water-based life forms. Wilson had been trying for years, and the closest he'd gotten was in Sulawesi when he'd managed to make a school of fish pause as they swam by him.

This morning, he headed west toward the distant Australian shore, that was just visible on the upper deck of the boat but invisible from the main. As he entered the water, he surrendered to the serene silence that surrounded him: he was just another animal in a sea full of animals. It wasn't long before he saw his first predation—a juvenile humphead wrasse working over a sea urchin among the staghorn coral. He was reminded of the Indian divers in Lakshadweep that referred to the "law of the sea" as opposed to the "law of the jungle." They'd argued that the jungle was quite tame compared to the violence of the oceans, and Wilson couldn't disagree. The ocean was giant web of prey and predator that made land-based food webs appear quite straightforward.

He surfaced momentarily to get eyes on the *Scuba Dreams III* and confirm his location before descending into the depths. He settled to the bottom with his back against a coral shelf, summoning his will in an attempt to lure anything that swam by his nook to come closer. *Think, think, think…* Using his will in this matter wasn't much different than fishing muddy waters for catfish; it was a game of patience.

After twenty minutes of letting his line loose, Wilson noticed something he'd never picked up on before—wherever he reeled out his will, the fish would subtly move to avoid swimming in its path at the last minute. Can the fish sense my magic? he considered.

He decided to test the hypothesis by sending out multiple threads and weaving his will together into a net, a feat in and of itself. Once Wilson was sure he could hold the shape with his mind, he waved it through the water, trying to catch one of the nearby bluestripe snappers schooling past. As the net glided, the fish dodged out of its way each time, as if it were a physical net. He tried a few more times to make sure it wasn't a fluke, and each time, the fish adjusted their trajectory to avoid intersection. It dawned on Wilson that he was going to have to rethink his strategy.

After the third failed attempt, he checked his pressure gauge out of habit and found he was down to 2,500 psi, significantly below what he anticipated if he were simply pleasure diving. He immediately left his perch and returned for the *Scuba Dreams III*, well within the safety range. After unloading his gear and arranging for his oxygen tanks to get topped off for the next dive, he took a seat on the covered middle deck for a bit more than a half hour, enjoying the pleasant weather with an Arnold Palmer that the ship's cook had whipped up for him.

He pondered his increased oxygen consumption; he disliked being caught unaware. He was generally so careful. It had been the first time he'd tried shaping his will into a net underwater; if human magic was air-based, that complex maneuver could account for the precipitous drop in his tanks, increasing his normal air consumption rates to something akin to heavy exercise, even though he wasn't winded in the slightest. He would have never noted the phenomena on dry land. Wilson then considered that the fish could be instinctually picking up the air implicit in his magic; evolutionarily speaking, it made sense for fish to have a natural aversion to air.

By the time Wilson had fully dried out, his tanks were ready for his second dive of the day, this time to the northeast. He needed more water in his magic net design and settled on a large sphere with a small opening at one end, like a fish trap made of his will. He moved the sphere about, but couldn't convince any fish to swim inside.

Still too much air, Wilson chided himself in frustration. He changed the sphere into a rectangular cuboid and spent ten minutes maneuvering an anemonefish into the open end. Once the fish was inside, Wilson "closed" the open side, trapping his target inside the box of his will. Wilson waited for the fish to make contact with one of the sides and complete his spell, but it stubbornly stayed in the center of the cube. He rapidly moved the box in hopes one of the sides would touch the fish, but it made compensatory adjustments and matched Wilson's speed.

Fine, two can play at that game. He concentrated and the box started to shrink. *Where you gonna swim now?* he mentally taunted his scaled opponent. When the box got to half its initial size, the anemonefish felt the approach of an unseen predator and reflexively darted toward its anemone. Unfortunately for the fish, it swam headlong into Wilson's will first.

He felt a surge of euphoria as the spell completed and he knew the fish was his. Even though he knew his charm was working, he outstretched his hand ever so carefully. He needed something from the fish, something exceedingly rare. The orange and white-striped fish drew closer and closer to Wilson's hand, stopping just inches away. It was then that Wilson threw the full force of his will toward the tiny, alien brain lurking between its two beady eyes, stunning it long enough for him to grab it, pull out his knife, and kill it. He skillfully ran the blade down the side of the fish, roughly scaling it. A cloud of scales emerged, and he plucked a handful and tucked them away in his waist pouch. The rest of the fish fell into a crevice in the coral; no doubt, a fortuitous meal for some hungry crustacean. That was the law of the sea: nothing went to waste.

Wilson had an inkling of how much magic he had used when he surfaced, high as a kite. Most magics—summoning being the main exception— had that effect on him, but there wasn't a way to summon a charmed fish; he had tried. Even buzzed, he kept his wits about him and located the *Scuba Dreams III*. Once he was safely on course, he allowed himself to fully enjoy it, swimming at a leisurely pace while he watched the beauty and horror of the raw nature below him.

Everyone was still out in the water when he returned and slipped his tank off, careful not to disturb the precious cargo in his waist pouch. The big grin on his face disappeared when one of the crewmembers informed him that his phone had been buzzing for the past half hour. He quickly toweled off before going back to his bunk and the private, locked drawer containing his personal items. Once he unlocked his phone, the first thing he checked was the light reader to see if the ambient light had changed since he'd placed it in the drawer—any change meant someone had opened the drawer, which would be useful information even if it didn't tell him who had opened the drawer.

The meter returned a negative, and now certain that his phone hadn't been tampered with while he was diving, he checked his messages; all six were from the Salt Mine. Wilson sighed. It had happened again—they were breaking into his vacation because he was the closest agent in the area.

Chapter Three

Honiara, Solomon Islands
8th of August, 11:35 p.m. (GMT+11)

The wheels of the A320 clutched at the wet runway of Honiara International Airport. Wilson wasn't the only passenger that felt a distinct rightward slip in the final deceleration, but all was forgiven when it landed safely. As much as he'd traveled, he'd never been to the Solomon Islands, and his general working knowledge was far from up-to-date. Sadly, most of what he knew of the Solomons concerned the Battle of Guadalcanal and the islands' strategic use in WWII. Because of this, he'd spent most of the flight over reading the CIA World Factbook's entry and anything of interest that he could scrounge up on the net during the flight over.

Even though he was in unknown environs, he stuck to a tested formula: exchange money, leave the airport, grab a cab. In his experience, if a nation's capital was attracting tourists, it had those things at all hours, even the places that were otherwise underdeveloped.

After a quick stop at the moneychanger, he left the airport and walked into the sultry night toward the all-to-familiar taxicab stand. True to form, the Salt Mine booking agents had already secured a room at the best hotel in Honiara, and Wilson took in his first sights of the island on the cab ride there. The scenery reminded him of a mix of Fiji and Vanuatu, and the breeze created by driving with the windows down filled his nostrils with cool sea air sweetened by the recent rains.

He exited the taxi, paying the cabbie with some of his new money; as part of the Commonwealth, the currency was colorful and featured a young Queen Elizabeth II. At check-in, he discovered the front desk clerk spoke English, a rare thing in the Solomon Islands, for although English was an official language, it was spoken by less than two percent of the population and there were more than seventy different indigenous languages. Wilson could only imagine how difficult it made governing and conducting bureaucratic business. As he collected his room keys, he inquired about where he could get a bite to eat this late, and was given the name and location of a nearby restaurant within walking distance.

Once inside his room, he assembled his Glock from its hidden compartment in his luggage, pulled on his dark clothing, and walked out the front door of the hotel into the night. His lodgings were only a few blocks away from the docks, currently occupied by his mission target: the *Hideki Maru*. Three days ago, it had been disabled while fishing the waters east of the islands and towed to the only dock in the Solomons that had a proper repair facility for a 150-ton ship. Wilson was tasked to investigate the nature of its incapacitation.

A breeze came in off the ocean, cooling the night with temperate gusts and rattling the leaves of the palm trees that lined the beach. As he followed the path toward the docks, he passed several groups of Islanders enjoying the evening with food, drink, music, conversation, and company. He couldn't understand what they were saying, but they left him alone as he passed by, which was what he really cared about.

He quickly sized up the shoddy security at the dock. Although it worked in his favor, he denounced it on general principle—any security job worth doing was worth doing right. The ten-foot chain link fence had barbed wire on the top, but there was a gap in the locked gate adjacent to the beachside vegetation that was big enough for a man to squeeze through. The only hitch was the prominent light right over the entrance in the otherwise poorly lit docks. He found a good rock and launched it at the light; it was easier than scaling barbed wire. The first throw missed, but his second didn't. He crouched low and waited for a few minutes to see if the popped light drew any attention before slipping through the gap.

No one seemed to care, so Wilson squeezed through the locked gate. He hugged the shadows as he crept along the small warehouses lining the docks until he found the *Hideki Maru*'s berth; it took him less than five minutes. Honiara was the capital of the Solomon Islands, but it was a relatively small city—less than a hundred thousand people—and its docks were correspondingly small. He watched the ship from cover to make sure there was no activity, and when nothing moved, he stealthily sidled alongside the boat and swung himself up and over in one smooth motion. Crouching against the solid metal deck railing, he paused again, double-checking if anyone was on board. As the silence settled, two distinct snores from the quarters in the superstructure could be heard. Wilson had figured as much—there was little reason to pay for a bed when you already had one aboard. They weren't a problem as long as they stayed asleep.

He gathered his will into a tight ball, making it ready on short notice, and crept toward the yawning blackness of the open door leading into the superstructure. The snores were louder at his approach, but not within the same room. He released a burst of light from his flashlight, and quickly closed his eyes so he could scan his retinal image for the stairs down without drawing undue attention from inside or outside the ship. If the incident on the *Hideki Maru* was the same type as the other five, the information he wanted would be in the engine room in the heart of the ship. It took a few tense moments and three more flashes of light to find the right door, but as he descended the snoring got quieter. Eventually, he felt it was safe enough to use more light.

The engine room was quiet; not even the generator was running. It bore the telltale signs that Wilson was looking for: small puddles of water everywhere indicated that the engine room had been flooded without evidence of structural failure.

He stepped over the tubes of the pump used to drain the room, collected a handful of water from one of the puddles, and brought it to his lips—it wasn't salty.

Water elementals, he thought to himself, *just like the others.* He quickly blew a puff out of his saltcaster, but as the white grains landed, they disintegrated into the water. *Well it's salty now*, he chided himself. He scanned for ways to double check his conclusion and went to the damp workbench. Picking up the soggy manual to the diesel engine, Wilson placed his tongue against the inside of the back cover: salt free as well.

He carefully made his way off the *Hideki Maru*, and stopped by the recommended restaurant for a quick bite on his way back to his hotel. He brought a bit back in a bag to secure his cover with the desk clerk. Not that anyone would care, but good tradecraft was good tradecraft. Once in his room, he sent a message regarding his findings on the *Hideki Maru*.

Wilson checked his Girard-Perregaux—Detroit would be just starting their day. He had no doubt they would send a lot of material once they processed his message, but there wasn't anything else he could do without knowing the full details. He settled for bed, and fell asleep to the rustling leaves of the palm tree outside the window of his fourth-floor room.

Chapter Four

Wilson lounged on his room's balcony facing north into Ironbottom Sound, enjoying a late breakfast of coffee, a few small rolls with butter and jam, and a papaya wedge. As predicted, the morning came with a full dossier which turned out to be remarkably thin. Five other vessels in the past eight months had been attacked at sea. Reports from each incapacitated ship stated that jostling impacts "insufficient to cause structural damage to the hull" immediately preceded the flooding of their engine room with fresh water.

The sailors who agreed to tell the full story—who were few, for fear of being labeled crazy—spoke of "water people" that boarded the ship, walked to the engine room, and disintegrated, leaving only water behind. In all of the encounters, the walking water had been indifferent to the sailors; they had ignored contact and did not return aggression to those sailors that futilely attacked them after they boarded the ship. Alas, the sailors' efforts had been in vain, as nothing seemed to faze the "water people." Everything slid smoothly through their aqueous bodies. The stories among those unwilling to believe their own eyes greatly varied. There was a healthy dose of rationalization, but the most common story was mumbles of mini-rogue waves. Wilson had seen it all too often—denying the unbelievable's very existence was how humanity coped.

While all the attacked ships were fishing boats on the smaller side—the largest was about 200 tons—that's where the similarities ended. No two ships flew under the same flag or were owned by the same person or parent company. They were attacked at different times in the course of sailing: two while actively fishing, two while traveling, and one while floating powerless as the engineer worked on replacing a blown hose.

The locations of the attacks varied as well. One occurred in the waters between Mauritius and Reunion, one west of Penang Island in the Malacca Strait, one south of the Channel Islands west of Los Angeles, one in the waters west of Cape Town, and the last one in the Indian Ocean twenty or so miles out from Mumbai. So far, the Mine's analysts had yet to find a pattern, and this recent attack didn't have any obvious points of concurrence with the previous five.

Wilson took a bite of papaya, and considered what he was up against as a flowery sweetness filled his mouth. Elementals were physical manifestations of an intellectual concept, similar to Plato's idea of the Platonic Forms. Water elementals were the *concept* of water made physical, and the traditional Western four—air, earth, fire, water—were just the tip of the iceberg. There were an amazing array of elementals, as many as there were ideas concerning the fundamental stuff that constituted the world. If people had thought about it, there could an elemental that embodied that contemplation.

Elementals weren't unintelligent, per se, but they lacked self-determination, relying upon others' direction for motivation. On the surface, they sounded like the perfect servants, but they had a tendency to go rogue—they would take instruction, but the longer they were manifested, the more they would glitch and slightly twist the intent of their directive. Educated practitioners were well aware of this flaw, and those that utilized elementals limited them to simple, one-time tasks before dismissing them.

Generally speaking, elementals were not naturally occurring and were almost always summoned. They *could* sometimes self-materialize in places of intense human stress, but it was extremely uncommon, and the chance of them doing so for similar repetitive attacks over an eight-month time frame was infinitesimal.

All of this added up to a puppet master pulling the strings, either a magician or a magical object. Wilson favored the later, as there were many more magical objects than there were practitioners, and new ones appeared from time to time without explanation or provenance. Some were enchanted by magicians trapping ghosts into items and using their essences to power the magic, but the vast majority of items simply blinked into existence. Even the Salt Mine was at a loss on the processes behind their spontaneous creation.

Wilson pushed away his empty breakfast plates, made another coffee, and started into the detailed files of each individual ship, beginning with the first attack and ending with the *Hideki Maru*. He familiarized himself with the special relationship Japan and the Solomon Islands had entered into, and committed the name and face of each of the sailors aboard the *Hideki Maru* to memory. If he was to pose as a reporter for the Institute of Tradition, he needed to get the basics right. Language was going to be a problem, as Wilson didn't speak Japanese or any of the languages of the Solomon Islands. He needed to track down either Tomohiro Tada, who spoke English, or Captain Takaharu Nakagawa, who spoke Russian.

Finished with his preparations, Wilson sipped his coffee and enjoyed the view of Ironbottom Sound. The water was absolutely crystal clear this morning and he wished that he had time to scuba. Past the shallows lurked more than two hundred ships and five hundred airplanes that had gone down during WWII. Diving deep amongst wrecked ships was one of his favorite things to do, and there were few places in the world with a greater concentration of shipwrecks than Ironbottom Sound.

As he daydreamed of deep waters, a beautiful megayacht floating nearly halfway between Honiara and Savo Island caught his eye. The idea of living on a ship instead of being landbound had always appealed to him, but it was rather incompatible with his work and not everyone had Clover's resources.

He retrieved his compact 12x50 binoculars and took a closer look. It was too far away to see the name, but from the elegantly projecting bow, it looked to be a newer Lürssen. If he had to guess, it was something within the past decade and close to 250 feet in length. *Maybe when I retire*, he mused. He passed his gaze to his quarry; through the binoculars the Honiara docks appeared gigantic and he spotted several sailors moving about the deck of the *Hideki Maru*.

*****

"Excuse me!" Wilson called out with a wave to the two Japanese men on the deck of the *Hideki Maru*. The two men stopped what they were doing and stared blankly at him.

"Excuse me," he repeated. "Is Tomohiro Tada aboard?" Their eyes lit up at the name, prompting a rapid exchange between them. The elder of the pair pointed to the city and said something in Japanese.

Quickly realizing the limitations of his Japanese and their English, Wilson tried a different tactic. "Is Captain Takaharu Nakagawa aboard?" Wilson asked in Russian, pretending not to recognize the captain.

"I am Captain Takaharu," the older man answered. His Russian was heavily accented but otherwise flawless and rapid. "What do you want?"

Wilson gave a small bow. "Captain Takaharu, I am Damon Warwick from the Institute of Tradition. We are a worldwide organization dedicated to preserving the knowledge of the past. I've heard of your recent encounter with the Water People when you were at sea," he answered, addressing the elementals by a generic name to put the captain at ease—of course everyone knew of the Water People!

The captain looked at his crewman and then down to the rope in his hand. "Whatever you have heard isn't true. We just suffered an engine failure. Nothing unusual happened," he dismissed the unwanted attention.

"Captain, I understand that is what you must say to others, but you don't have to say it to me. I know all about the Water People; they knock about fishing vessels, come aboard, and drown engine compartments. Your ship isn't the only one," Wilson reassured him.

"You understand nothing. Leave us be," the captain responded resolutely before delivering a small speech in Japanese to the other sailor.

"I've seen them myself," Wilson interrupted once the younger sailor started his reply. "They're made of fresh water, no?"

The captain held up his hand, silencing his crewman. He turned his dark steely eyes on Wilson, assessing the measure of him. "Who are you again?"

"Damon Warwick from the Institute of Tradition. We

believe that our elders held knowledge that we've surrendered, and we seek to bring that knowledge back," Wilson answered slowly and deliberately, keeping his posture deferential to the captain. In his experience, Asian cultures valued respect and reacted poorly to being cornered into a particular stance. In negotiations, he always allowed a path to save face.

The captain appraised the strange man before him and Wilson was pleased when he grunted, "Come aboard."

At first, the captain was hesitant to speak, but Wilson eventually got the full incident out of him with an offer to pay for the exclusive story; the extra money would make up some of the fishing shortfall and save face among any crew that disapproved of sharing the tale. Once Takaharu started, he couldn't stop. Wilson had seen it before: the desperate need to unburden oneself of something unfathomable was an act bordering on the confessional. When the extraordinary happened to a person, having someone who was willing to believe them was everything.

Wilson nodded sympathetically, changing his facial expressions every so often and gasping in shock at the apex. While the sailors of the *Hideki Maru* had a better chance of winning the lottery than of ever encountering another water elemental, he recommended that the captain keep some vinegar on deck to throw at the Water People should he ever encounter them again. It wasn't a guaranteed defense, but they usually fled before it even in very small concentrations. There was a long list of various things water elementals didn't like, but the most effective substances—pure sodium, potassium, or any other alkali metal—were unwise to use when you were surrounded by water. At least vinegar wouldn't explode on the sailors if it got wet.

Wilson thanked him for his account and left the *Hideki Maru*, a thousand dollars poorer. When he returned to his hotel room, he texted his report to the Salt Mine. It wasn't much, but it added to the body of evidence. Eventually a pattern would emerge and something could be done about the problem. Until then, collecting data was all that was possible.

He took lunch on his covered balcony where he could enjoy the sun without getting burned. The yacht he'd admired that morning had moved closer; now he could see its name through his binoculars—*Lady Alexandra*. After a quick search on the web, he discovered it was the 157th largest yacht in the world; he'd even got the shipbuilder right. Pleased as punch, he searched for scuba tours out of Honiara. He still had a week of vacation left, and he wanted to get a few good dives in before flying back to Australia.

Chapter Five

Nemo Sea Laboratory, West of Sal Island, Cape Verde
11th of August, 11:47 p.m. (GMT-1)

Andrei Vasilovich Zarubin lay in his bunk, waiting for the others to fall asleep. Like a white-noise machine, the mechanical drone of the air supply engines generated a persistent hum as air was brought from the surface, compressed, and released one hundred feet beneath the waves into the Nemo Sea Laboratory. All aboard knew the innovative research facility was an autonomous underwater habitat, capable of maneuvering itself vertically and horizontally with cables connecting it to the surface and its own air and energy reserves, but that knowledge would do little to stem the tension that would erupt should the humming suddenly stop. The brainchild of programmer, business mogul, and futurist Karl Lundqvist, Nemo Lab was built to be the world's premier underwater scientific nexus and test bed. The Swede believed that the oceans were the keystone for humanity's future, and he'd dedicated a portion of his vast wealth to demonstrate his opinions.

It was this wealth that made him a target for extortion by the Ivory Tower. Unfortunately, getting inside his organization had proven impossible, which was why Zarubin had spent the past four months underwater, crammed between a pair of decommissioned Russian Whisky-class submarines that supported the structure built between them. Lundqvist had opened the entire lab to the scientific community, except for one of the sub bodies reserved for his own personal pursuits—that was off limits to all but Lundqvist's closest confidents. After considering their options, the Interior Council had sent in Zarubin under the alias of Myroslav Skliar, a Ukrainian scientist who'd fled Sevastopol after the Russians annexed it. The alias had been good enough to book him a bunk in the Nemo Sea Laboratory; if infiltration of Lundqvist's actual organization wasn't possible, the next best thing was being adjacent to his operations.

Establishing the extortion of Lundqvist was Zarubin's first open-ended assignment; his prior four had been short and specific. A crash course in scuba and marine biology had been adequate to avoid attracting attention, and he'd breezed through the first two weeks of his six-month schedule in the Nemo Lab, culminating in the compulsory psychological surface that everyone did. The Nemo Lab may have been huge compared with prior underwater labs, but it was still cramped and packed with people and equipment. Not everyone could handle it, and having a set escape after two weeks prevented difficulties down the line. Researchers who'd found they couldn't continue could call it quits and get a refund on the remainder of their booked time, no questions asked.

Zarubin's problems hadn't started until later; living and working in such close quarters made feigning a mastery of marine biology challenging. No matter how much he increased his knowledge on the subject in which he was supposedly an expert, he'd hadn't managed to shake the fear of exposure. It pressed on him like the unrelenting water that constantly lurked just outside the thin metal hull of the laboratory.

Despite the precarious nature of his assignment, he had pressed on, using his wits, charm, and a little bit of magic to make friends and contacts for future exploitation. Over time, he'd wormed his way in socially with those in the Nemo that operated within Lundqvist's organization, and for the first time in months, everything was going as planned.

Then, two days ago, Zarubin had stumbled upon what Lundqvist was really doing and knew he had to escape—*really* escape. Simply leaving the Nemo, traveling to Sal Island, and then catching a plane to Moscow wouldn't work. He needed to disappear and he needed to completely cover his tracks. He needed to destroy the laboratory.

Always have an exit plan. It had been drilled into him during his GRU training and reinforced once he'd been picked up by the Ivory Tower and introduced to the real world: the realm of magic and the power of will. Assessing his surroundings and its security had been the first thing he did upon his arrival at Nemo Sea Laboratory. During his first surface, he'd feigned a toothache to buy some additional time on land, and he'd returned to the sea lab with a six-pack of one-ounce tubs of knock-off Play-Doh. They had been a big hit with the other crewmembers, and if the smell, color, or texture were slightly off, it was easily chalked up to them being a generic version— no one suspected that they were actually colored and scented C4, designed to be hidden in plain sight. Those six tubs were far and away enough to drown the Nemo, especially if placed in six different structurally important locations.

Once Zarubin had decided to implement his most-severe escape scenario, he'd sent out a coded message via his normal communications and received word that the *Yantar*, one of the Russian Navy's vessels, would be waiting for him tonight three miles due west. All he had to do now was set the charges, steal one of the Nemo's minisubs, and be at the appointed coordinates.

He took a deep breath to slow his racing heart. It was almost time, he was just waiting for Colcheck's snore. All his cabinmates used earplugs because of it, and if they could soundly sleep through that racket, Zarubin would be in the clear. He hated undoing all his soft target groundwork—he'd put a lot of time and effort into charming the various crewmembers of the Nemo—but it was the only way to ensure he was the only one who knew the secret. He fondled the memory stick that he'd kept on his person for the past two days. He consoled himself that the reward he would receive from the Ivory Tower for his efforts would easily outstrip anything he would have earned from a percentage of the average extortion scheme, even from a target as wealthy as Karl Lundqvist.

Eventually, the rhythmic rumble of nasal turbulence rattled and echoed against the metal walls of the cabin. Once he was sure everyone was down, he carefully snuck out of his sleeping quarters and purloined from the diving supplies a waterproof pouch for the memory stick, placing it back in his silk neck pouch after ensuring it was sealed. After closing the supply closet, he suddenly worried that he'd done something wrong, so he reopened it and grabbed another waterproof pouch and double-bagged the memory stick. Calmed, he continued with his plan.

The hum of the ventilation engines grew louder as he entered his part of the lab, located near the services section; in addition to pulling air from the surface, the Nemo was largely powered by a floating platform composed of solar panels that topped off the batteries before nighttime energy consumption started. He opened the drawer under his desk and grabbed his C4 and the detonators. The detonators were disguised as a twelve pack of pencils and they were completely functional, but their butt ends packed more than just an eraser.

He separated the detonators from the casings and placed his first charge against the bottom of one of the large borosilicate glass windows. Once the charge was set, he removed a safety tab and twisted four complete rotations on the detonator, triggering a ten-minute countdown before the compact explosive within went off.

Now on an unalterable timeline, he raced to the other five locations he'd carefully preselected and placed a charge at each. *Always know how you're getting out,* Zarubin's mind kept repeating as he worked. Once all the charges were placed, he climbed to the top of Nemo Lab, which jutted off of the main body of the structure, forming the moon pool they used for launching the minisubs. The first time he'd heard of a moon pool, he found it very counterintuitive that anyone would cut a hole into a perfectly good air-filled underwater building, but without it, there was no easy way for people and goods to get in and out.

Zarubin checked his watch and picked up his pace. This was the trickiest part, but if he worked rapidly, his inevitable noise shouldn't wake anyone. It took less than a minute for him to drop one of DeepWorker 2000 minisubs, climb in, and close the hatch behind him. He'd scheduled use of the sub in the course of his research just for this very contingency.

He slid into the pilot seat and moved his hands over the controls; the electric engine started up immediately, and he steered the sub clear of Nemo Lab. Once he was headed dead west, he hit the accelerator for all it was worth. Intellectually, he knew the water would absorb the shockwaves of the explosions and he didn't need to be that far way to avoid harm, but his gut wanted as much distance as possible—not only for his own protection, but for his conscience. He would rather not be reminded that he just ensured the death of thirty-five innocent scientists.

*****

The *Yantar* was a special purpose vessel in the Russian Navy with a displacement of 5,736 tons and a length of 354 feet. As a special purpose vessel, its primary mission was to protect the secrets of Mother Russia, and it did that by functioning as a mothership to a pair of minisubs with an operational depth of 20,000 feet. Most notably, it had recently made the news recovering sensitive parts from two downed fighter planes—a Su-33 and a MiG-29—in the eastern Mediterranean, as well as searching for the downed Argentinian sub ARA-*San Juan* off the coast of Argentina.

It was also renowned in intelligence circles for hanging around the coast of Cuba near Guantanamo Bay, as well as off the coast of Israel. For regardless what was officially said, the *Yantar* was really designed for spying. Its two subs and cadre of remote-operated vehicles performed deep-water engineering missions, including cutting undersea cables, tapping undersea cables, and delousing—the colloquial term used to describe removing another country's tap on an undersea cable. There was a constant underwater battle for information and the *Yantar* was one of Russia's front-line fighters.

Petty Officer Boris Mikhailovich Petrov was manning the

communications screen when the flashing red light indicated a high-priority message that demanded his immediate attention— IMMEDIATE MANEUVER 16°48'28.4"N 23°02'55.2"W MISSION CRITICAL – ADD INFO PENDING. Normally, he would have relayed a message over the intercom, but one didn't use comms for a MISSSION CRITICAL.

Once read, he clicked the print icon, tore the slip of paper off the printer, and raced out of communications to hand deliver the message to the captain, who was in the ROV launch and recovery control tower on the stern of the ship. It was a brisk run—a little under a hundred yards—but as it involved traveling down three decks and then back up three decks, he was taking in full breaths from the exertion when he finally arrived. Captain Nikolai Gusev took the slip of paper from Petrov's hands, read the message, and with a quick nod to the petty officer, he ordered the just-launched ROV back to the surface. Within twenty minutes, the *Yantar* was on its way to its newly ordered destination.

Since receiving the MISSION CRITICAL, *Yantar* had spent the past fifty-five hours on a beeline to Cape Verde. Its sudden movement had attracted a lot of attention from those tasked with tracking spy vessels, and when it finally stopped off the coast of Sal Island, Cape Verde, several brains around the world puzzled—what prompted a Russian spy ship to travel two days at full power, and why weren't they in the know?

While dozens of people in the intelligence community

frantically looked for answers and connections, there was one who was unruffled. She sat at her no-nonsense desk beneath at least 300 feet of salt looking at the high-quality reproduction of *The Temptation of Saint Anthony* by Jan Brueghel the Elder that hung on her wall. She often consulted the work after making a hard decision. She sipped a cognac and waited for the dominos to fall, admiring his use of contrast and color. *I wonder what Jan would think if he knew I'd be still admiring his work four hundred years later?*

Chapter Six

Yantar, West of Sal Island, Cape Verde
12th of August, 12:39 a.m. (GMT-1)

Petty Officer Boris Mikhailovich Petrov closely watched *Yantar*'s medium-frequency sonar array screen, searching for any sign of the mini-submarine they were supposed to rescue. He nervously tapped his fingers along the dagger tattoo on his left forearm. Technically, he wasn't supposed to know who they were picking up, nor why, but Petrov—ever curious about what was going on with his ship—had snuck in some furtive glances at communications not intended for his eyes. He was wary of the impending arrival of Zarubin and would be glad when the *Yantar*—and by proxy, himself—was done with his business and could return to the proverbial shadows.

The explosions at Nemo Sea Laboratory had occurred more than half an hour earlier, and the captain and lieutenant hovered over him as he bent toward the screen, expectantly anticipating the first outline of the minisub.

A tiny silhouette appeared on the edge of the screen. "There!" Petrov excitedly pointed.

"Are you sure?" the captain asked, looking over the petty officer's shoulder.

"Not a hundred percent," he pulled back his enthusiasm to a professional level, "but it's exactly where it should be."

The captain nodded and they waited in silence while Petrov checked a few more metrics. Less than a minute later, Petrov declared, "Now I'm certain, Captain. That's our target."

Captain Gusev clapped a congratulatory hand on Petrov's shoulder and ordered the ship to ready for its new arrival. Despite its speedy journey, the trip south had been largely uneventful, with the exception of readying the massive side hanger used to pick up minisubs. Before the *Yantar* could pick up any incoming subs, it had to first clear out the current occupant in the hanger: the AS-37 *Rus*. The AS-37 *Rus* was almost thirty feet long and displaced twenty-five tons. Moving it about the deck wasn't an easy task. It required a lot of muscle power and was simply impossible to do on a rolling deck. Thankfully, they'd hit half a day of clear seas during their final approach, and the AS-37 *Rus* was now lashed to the deck, leaving room for Zarubin's much smaller DeepWorker 2000.

Petrov continued to watch the slow approach of the minisub on the screen until a cry from outside announced the sub had surfaced. The petty officer walked outside communications to the upper deck and looked east toward the distant lights of Sal Island. Telling distance on the dark ocean waters was difficult, but the single flashing red light blinking in the darkness looked about a quarter mile away, and it was bobbing with the familiar rhythm of the water. The *Yantar* turned one of its powerful searchlights toward the incoming object, revealing a rocking orange submarine sturdily making its way to the larger ship.

The process of retrieving a submarine was straightforward, and the crew of the *Yantar* had it down to muscle memory. First, the hanger doors opened, and the launching crane slowly extended out over the water. With the turn a wheel, the operator lowered the central cylinder to make initial contact via the latch hook that would attach to the top of the submarine. Once the sub was hooked by a brave seaman—attached by safety ties to the central cylinder—the four curved hydraulic arms branching off each side of the central cylinder would contract around the body of the sub, securing it in its padded grasp and locking the sub and crane into one unit to prevent any swinging, twisting, or turning in mid-air. Only then was the crane retracted and the sub pulled out of the water and onto the *Yantar*.

Petrov didn't know if the operator of the sub was informed of what he was supposed to do, but having a giant crane hanging out of the side of the ship didn't take much explanation. The DeepWorker 2000 slid under the crane and popped its canopy. "Hello! It's nice to see you!" Zarubin yelled out with a wave once the top was free. The seaman on the crane returned the greeting and informed him of the craning process.

It wasn't the ideal way to learn, but Zarubin enthusiastically played his part, ecstatic to see fellow humans after nearly an hour of nothing but the vast wet blackness of the ocean. He ran the latching hook's guy-wire through the DeepWorker 2000's hard point and called back to the seamen on the central cylinder. Once they were sure the hook was guided, they lowered it and attached it to the hard point. After double-checking the connection, Zarubin closed the canopy and waited for the crane and the seaman of the *Yantar* to do their work.

Petrov observed from his perch until the sub disappeared into the hanger. He then returned to his station, monitoring all the communications coming and going on the *Yantar*.

*****

Captain Gusev paused in the doorway of the side hanger; he believed in giving his men space to work, especially when it involved moving parts and heavy machinery. Once he heard the distinctive click of the crane locking into place and the hanger was cleared, he entered and waited for their new passenger to free himself.

As soon as the acrylic dome was up, he introduced himself, "I am Captain Gusev. Welcome aboard the *Yantar*."

The captain watched his guest struggle to free himself from the sub and eventually push out his hand. "Hello, Captain. I am Senior Lieutenant Andrei Zarubin. I assume you have had a full briefing on what we're to do next?"

The captain shook his hand. "Yes, I have." He looked at his watch. "Once we get you settled, we are to return to Reka

Zapadnaya Litsa." Zapadnaya Litsa was the naval base for the Russian Northern Fleet. It was on the Kola Peninsula, twenty or thirty kilometers west of Murmansk.

"How long will that be?" Zarubin asked as he roughly dragged his meager belongings—all stuffed into large orange water-resistant bag—out of the sub and onto the deck.

"No more than twelve days."

Zarubin cursed. "That's too long. I have to get back quicker than that. What is the nearest city with a major airport?"

"Presumably one that doesn't belong to a country you just attacked?" Captain Gusev clipped out; he wasn't pleased with Zarubin's oily demeanor.

"Of course," Zarubin blithely responded.

"Dakar, Senegal," the captain responded. "I believe we could be there in a little more than a day."

"Then that's where we're going," Zarubin insisted.

"I'll need to consult before changing course," Gusev countered. "There were no orders indicating that you were to have a say in where my ship goes."

"There should have been," Zarubin affirmed, patting his silk passport pouch that hung around his neck that held the double-bagged memory stick. "What I have is of the utmost importance to the security of our great nation."

The captain bit his tongue and simply nodded in response. "Seaman Koshkin," he ordered the nearest sailor. "Show the lieutenant—"

"Senior lieutenant," Zarubin corrected.

"...*senior* lieutenant to his quarters and then escort him to the bridge in half an hour."

"Yes, Captain!"

"I'd like to stop by the mess for a coffee on the way," Zarubin requested. Seaman Koshkin looked to the captain, who nodded his approval before heading to communications. On the way, Captain Gusev made some colorful remarks about Zarubin's impertinence to himself before reframing the problem before him as something from which he could benefit.

His decision was made by the time he climbed the three sets of stairs leading to the bridge and then communications— he would send word to Fleet Headquarters inquiring about the destination change, but start immediately for Dakar anyway. If they replied favorably, he would appear decisive; if they rebuked the change in plans, he had enough pull to put the blame entirely on the senior lieutenant. *After all*, he thought, *the Yantar had been ordered to sail at full speed for two days to rendezvous with Zarubin*; no one could fault its captain for thinking the mission of the highest importance.

His confident stride carried him over the threshold and he ordered the communications petty officer, "Petrov, send a message to Saint Petersburg. Our guest believes that whatever's around his neck is important enough to give him the authority to determine our destination. Ask HQ if this is the case. He wishes us to go to Dakar. When you get an answer, find me on the bridge. I'm ordering us to Dakar until we get confirmation otherwise."

Petrov nodded and the captain left once he was sure communication had been established, figuring it would probably take several hours to receive the answer.

The *Yantar* had been underway at full speed toward Dakar for less than ten minutes when Petrov entered the bridge, slip of paper in hand. Caption Gusev's first thought was, *I must have guessed correctly*, at the sight of the petty officer on the bridge. He took the offered slip and read, OFFER ALL ASSISTANCE – CONFIRM ANY FUTURE CHANGES. MISSION CRITICAL.

He dismissed the waiting Petrov with a nod and looked starboard onto the dark shores of northwestern Sal Island. Although he couldn't see it in the night, he'd sailed by it several times in his life. It was a dry and barren place, and most of its shoreline along the north was igneous cliff faces, rising ten feet or more from the high-tide water line. There were no population centers on the northern part of the island, and the only light was from the occasional recreational campfire started on the few sandy beaches accessible from the cliffs. *Tiny candles in a world of darkness*, he reflected.

Petrov was on his way back to communications when the *Yantar* fearfully shuddered. Were he and the captain not looking that direction, they would have sworn another large ship had crashed into the *Yantar*'s starboard. The petty officer struggled to maintain his balance but lost it, and force of the unexpected shift sent him clawing over the railing and down to the middle deck.

The scream from his landing wasn't the only yell of pain rolling out of the ship; the crew in the bridge was knocked out of their seats, and the navigator fell limp after taking a nasty head wound against the pole of the conning officer's chair. It was worse below decks, where heads and wrists, elbows and ankles all suffered under the sudden jostling. As the seas had been calm, no one was prepared for it.

Captain Gusev immediately regained his footing and looked starboard at the open sea to double-check that he was right. Nothing had changed with the view he had just been admiring. He grabbed his radio and switched it to communications. "Status report!"

The comm crackled. "No threats detected, Captain!"

"Something just hit us, what the hell was it?" he demanded as the conning officer bent over the navigator, checking on the head wound. When he raised his hands they were covered with blood, but the captain was already in motion, unlocking the first aid kit with one hand and sliding it along the floor to the kneeling officer. Once the kit was out of his hand, the captain instinctively grabbed hold of the nearby handhold. He had spent more than two decades at sea, and his unconscious instinct was to steady himself in unusual situations.

With his other hand, he raised the radio back to his mouth.

"Whales?" he grasped for possibilities. "Did we hit a whale?" A whale impact shouldn't have had such force, but he was at a loss as to what had happened.

"No signs of biologics within range, Captain."

Surely it couldn't be a sub? "Any submarines detected?" It should have been impossible for them to hit a submarine, but if it had been dormant, or perhaps even blindly rising—a stupid thing to do—the *Yantar* could have been unlucky enough to win the shit-lottery.

Before comms could respond, the *Yantar* took another hit. This impact was worse than the first, and from the port. Once more, the crew lurched off their feet and banged against various metal surfaces of the ship. Only the reflexive bracing of the captain kept him from rolling along with the majority of the crew.

Who is attacking my ship?!

*****

Already knocked to the ground by the first impact, Senior Lieutenant Zarubin rolled and slammed his hip on one of the raised support ribs on the starboard wall of his quarters as the second impact hit the *Yantar*. *I've got to get to shore*, he thought, massaging his hip. *They've got a bead on me!* He raised himself from the metal floor and looked out into the corridor, finding Seaman Koshkin limp and unconscious. The seaman had hit his head against one of the metal braces on the first shudder, and the second had tossed him along the floor, leaving a smear of blood and an impact splash.

Fearing the worst, Zarubin ran down the corridor and outside onto the main deck. Along the superstructure were a series of metal bins that contained what he needed: an inflatable life raft. If he could get to a small-enough craft, he could set up wards against the water elementals attacking the ship, just like he'd done in the minisub. If they couldn't sense him, they couldn't hurt him. He never thought they'd be able to attack a ship almost as big as two hockey rinks, nevertheless attack with such effect.

Zarubin had only taken a few steps when the ship was rammed again. But this time, instead of a one-directional blow, he could see the bow had twisted clockwise while the stern twisted counterclockwise, as if the water had solidified and was trying to shear the *Yantar* abeam. Screeching metal drowned out the shouts of the seamen, and just as suddenly quieted. The dreadful sound of rushing water filled the downward stairwells. Both the bow and the stern started pitching upward as water rushed into the midship.

Recognizing the rushing water as the death-knell of the *Yantar*, Zarubin propelled himself to the bins. Next to the bins containing the life rafts was Petty Officer Petrov, who'd just fallen down the flight of stairs to the main deck after hopping up them on his non-injured leg. The second hit had sent him tumbling, and it was only dumb luck that had kept his broken leg from taking another collision on the way down.

"The ship is doomed! Grab the extra life rafts," the petty officer yelled. "We'll inflate them once we're on the water and rescue the others."

It wasn't precisely what Zarubin had in mind, but he went along with it—he'd take care of Petrov later. The senior lieutenant grabbed three inflatable rafts while the petty officer grabbed one and hopped to the main deck's railing, which had already dropped several feet toward the waterline. Petrov visibly readied himself and rolled over the high railing into the warm tropical waters. He tried to dive as best he could to avoid putting additional pressure on his broken leg, but he still screamed from the impact as he hit.

Once the spike of pain subsided to the point where he could think clearly, Petrov inflated the raft. Zarubin climbed in as soon as he could, depositing three additional rafts in the center. Petrov clumsily followed, protecting his leg from damage as much as he could. Behind them, the *Yantar* continued its descent. It had already sunk a few more feet down, and it wouldn't take more than a minute or two before it disappeared forever, resting on the quiet sea floor two hundred fifty feet below.

Petrov tore into the equipment bag, extracted the interlocking pieces of the sectional paddle, and started putting them together. Once the paddle was assembled, he'd launch the additional inflatables and moor them all together.

As he worked, Zarubin closed his eyes, summoned his will, and started humming. Amidst the chaos, the droning note caught Petrov's attention, and when he looked up, he noticed the outline of a travel pouch on Zarubin's chest, tightly clinging to his torso underneath his wet clothes. Once the paddle clicked into place, Petrov turned his attention back to the *Yantar* just in time to see one of his fellow seaman dragged under the waves by what looked to be a figure made entirely of water.

"What the hell?" he yelled. "Did you see that?"

Zarubin kept his eyes closed and kept humming.

Petrov looked for other survivors and again, saw one of his comrades dragged into the deep by a watery figure. "Dammit, Zarubin, what the hell is that?"

"Shut up! I'm concentrating to keep us safe. Paddle to land if you want to live," he commanded.

Broken-legged and surrounded by terrifying things, Petrov did as ordered. He crawled to get behind Zarubin and started paddling for all he was worth. Looking over his shoulder as he paddled, he watched the entire complement of the *Yantar* dragged down even as the ship itself sank beneath the waves. He quickly fell into a rhythm where he no longer had to think about paddling and instead concentrated on Zarubin, probing his song with his will. The senior lieutenant was so preoccupied with keeping the elementals at bay that he failed to notice the subtle magic that was not his own.

Once Petrov was confident he'd identified the magic at work, he ran his fingers over the knife tattoo on his forearm and summoned it off the surface and into his hand. Zarubin died almost instantly when the NR-40 knife slid between his ribs and into his heart. The last thing he heard was the tinkling sound of Petrov's will picking up the enchantment before it stopped.

Once he was sure Zarubin was dead, Petrov retrieved the neck pouch and liberated anything else in the dead man's pockets. He pulled the knife out of his back, wiped the blade on Zarubin's clothes, and tossed the body off the raft. There were no other survivors of the *Yantar*—the water elementals had seen to that—and no one would know Petty Officer Boris Mikhailovich Petrov wasn't among their number.

As he hummed, Petrov looked toward the dark and barren north shore of Sal Island, less than a mile away. It was time for him to come in out of the cold. It had been five long years in Russia, and it was time for Alexander James Husnik—Salt Mine codename Stigma—to go home.

Chapter Seven

Wilson drove down the dusty dirt road in his all-wheel-drive vehicle, loaded with plenty of water, food, and supplies. When he'd originally decided to obtain some soil from the center of Australia, it seemed like an innocuous task…until he found out there were five centers of the continent, depending on how one measured. Rather than wager a guess and risk being wrong, Wilson sided with caution and planned on making five stops on his trip into the dry and barren center of the Land Down Under.

He'd taken a series of flights from the Solomon Islands into Alice Springs, using the layovers and airtime to catch up on current events; even on vacation, Wilson kept up with international news. It was more than an exercise of good tradecraft or a force of habit; in his line of work, he never knew when the disaster of the day was going to become his next assignment.

Initially, Wilson had paid little heed to the explosion at Nemo Sea Laboratory. As a diver and an enthusiast, he'd heard of the self-sufficient underwater habitat in passing, but it didn't take a genius to figure out humans weren't made to live below the waterline. However, his interest grew once he read out about the *Yantar*'s disappearance in nearby waters. He knew of the Russian spy ship by reputation, and how closely it was watched by the intelligence community; if the Russians were letting the rest of the world know it was MIA, it meant they really didn't know what had happened to it. When he'd checked the news at the next layover and read about the remains of the Russian ship destroyed at sea, Wilson knew something big was happening and wished he had access to his dailies to get the real story.

The harsh sun beat down on the dry land as he followed his phone's directions to the geodetic median point, the first of the so-called centers of Australia, and pulled his vehicle as far to the side of the road as possible. There wasn't much traffic, but he saw little reason to tempt fate. A quick check on his phone revealed the next twist in the tale: Russia was now blaming the sinking of the *Yantar* on Myroslav Skliar, a Ukrainian national who happened to be one of the visiting scientists at the sea lab. Apparently, the Russian Navy reported they'd received a distress signal from Skliar, who claimed to have escaped the destruction of the Nemo by using one of the minisubs. As the only ship in the area, the *Yantar* had rescued him in good faith, only to disappear under the waves within less than an hour of picking up the Ukrainian. Wilson shook his head; he didn't know what really happened, but he was pretty sure that whoever crafted this report was missing their calling as a screenwriter.

His phone rang as he was watching a video of the Russian ambassador to Cape Verde delivering a speech about the need for Cape Verde to fully investigate Ukrainian espionage in their territory. It was Alicia Moncrief, the Salt Mine agent codenamed Clover. Intrigued, he picked up instead of letting it go to voicemail.

"Alicia," Wilson answered as a way of greeting.

"Wilson!" she exclaimed, caught off guard to speak to him directly instead of leaving a message. "I'm sorry to bother you on your vacation, but I have some news I thought you'd appreciate finding out as soon as possible." Her voice sounded unusually thin and rose in tone at the end, like she was asking a question even though she wasn't.

"How did you know I was on vacation?" he quizzed her.

"It may have come up during a situation room, but no worries, that's all settled now," she glossed over the details nonchalantly.

"Is that what you called to tell me—I missed a situation room?" he asked drily.

"No, silly," she disregarded his tone. "I called to tell you Stigma's alive." She remained uncharacteristically quiet, uncertain if this was good news, bad news, or even news to Wilson.

"Alex is alive?" Wilson inquired incredulously. His stomach fell as he spoke the words; somehow saying them aloud made them more real.

"Yes," she averred. "Can you believe it? I'd have killed him if I wasn't sent to rescue him! He was stranded in the middle of nowhere and couldn't access normal channels, so Leader had me pick him up." It wasn't the first time she'd been sent to bail out a fellow agent; she'd earned her codename honestly. Over the years, she'd helped Wilson on several missions, and her unparalleled mobility never failed to bring some stability to a chaotic scene. Being a near-billionaire had its benefits.

Although rattled by the information, Wilson managed to keep his voice calm and casual. "What's he been up to?" As soon as the words left his mouth, his brain put two and two together. "Wait, let me guess—something about a spy ship and an underwater laboratory?"

"Don't know," she confessed. Wilson could almost hear the pout on the other end of the line. Moncrief, who had more than enough money, traded in the currency of favors and information, and there was little that annoyed her more than being left out of the loop. "Neither he nor Leader saw fit to fill me in at the time, but I *did* retrieve him from Cape Verde," she insinuated. She waited for him to say something, and when the silence grew too thick for her to bear any longer, she added apologetically, "I would have called sooner but they just rescinded the internal gag order on his return."

The news slowly sunk in, and Wilson's mind was spinning all manner of possibilities. "Protocol is protocol," he responded neutrally. "Thanks for the heads up. If you get a chance, tell him I said hello and that he's a royal bastard."

Her airy high-pitched laugh filled the line. "And rob you of the pleasure? I'll let you tell him yourself. Enjoy the rest of your vacation," she called out before Wilson had a chance to cut the line. He stepped out of the car, grabbed the first handful of Australian soil, and moved onto the next set of coordinates in search for the true center.

Wilson was thankful he'd mapped out a circuit before he'd left his hotel this morning. It allowed him to drive on autopilot and mindlessly obey his GPS while he processed Alex's resurrection after all these years. He had all these moving parts that operated under the assumption that Alex was gone that suddenly all had to be reconfigured. When the voice on his phone told him he was at his next destination, he methodically retrieved a sample of red dirt to add to the collection and proceeded to the next site.

Eventually, he found himself at the Lambert center, the last center of the continent on his route. As he bent over to grab the final handful of Australian soil, he nearly fell over. He caught himself and reflexively looked around to see if anyone had seen him stumble, which he immediately recognized as ridiculous. There wasn't anyone within miles of the plaque and flag that marked the site—it had been a twelve-mile drive down a dirt road that was tagged with a "4WD ONLY" sign that was somehow in worse condition than the road had been.

Wilson ran his dry tongue over his chapped lips—when

was the last time he drank something? He dusted off his hands and returned to his SUV, reaching into the back for a bottle of water and slaking his thirst. Ever since he'd gotten Moncrief's call, memories he had long considered buried kept bubbling to the surface: Istanbul, Berlin, and worst of all, Utashinai.

He and Alex had been sent to the small city in the mountains of Hokkaido to deal with an infestation of karakuras summoned by Arzum Kazaz, a Turkish magician seeking revenge against the hospital where her husband had died after a skiing accident in the Hidaka Mountains. Grief made people do odd things. By the time they'd cornered and dispatched Kazaz in one of the abandoned coal mines, the demons had killed more than a dozen people.

That should have been the end of it; her death should have sent the karakuras back to the shadow realm, but it hadn't. As professionals, he and Alex had been loaded out properly, and their bullets were banishing the demons as intended, but they hadn't counted on the instability of the rock surrounding them. Forty years of Hokkaido earthquakes had taken a toll on the mine's corridors, and neither had been prepared when the ceiling came down because of the vibrations of their weapons and separated them—Alex on one side with the flashlight, and Wilson on the other in the dark with the majority of the remaining shadow demons.

By the time Alex had circled around and found him, Wilson was already wandering off the mortal coil into the land of the dead, but he was never to arrive. Somehow, Alex had latched ahold of Wilson's spirit and forced it back into his broken body. Then, he'd *healed* Wilson's body enough to sustain its tie to its spirit.

Which was impossible—or more accurately, had been considered impossible. Magic doesn't heal flesh; it's one of the first things new practitioners learn. If a magician tries to heal someone, they only end up giving themselves the same injury. If they try to heal themselves, they end up in the same state they started, but with a new karmic burden as if they'd been successful. By all rights, it shouldn't have worked, but Wilson had been alive, and even conscious, for the rendezvous with Moncrief for their airlift out.

When they'd returned to the Salt Mine, Stigma's "miracle" became a point of contention. Chloe and Dot had been baffled and raised quite the fuss when they read Alex's report. They didn't believe him and it didn't help that Alex couldn't explain how he did it, nor could he reproduce it. A lot could be said about magic, much of it complaints and criticisms, but it was repeatable. Wilson, on the other hand, had taken it in stride. He'd spent a fair amount of time dealing with magic that wasn't functioning as it was supposed to, and he'd place his "miracle" into the broad category of "things I hate about my job."

It had taken him nearly half a year to fully recover from his injuries. Alex may have healed him enough that he didn't die in the collapsed mine, but his efforts appeared to retard his natural healing processes as an unintended side effect. During his long recovery, he'd been rather un-Wilson-like in his behavior. Everyone chalked it up to the near-death experience and the frustration at his magically prolonged convalescence, so they didn't press him on the matter. It took Wilson a long time to figure out what had really changed, and when he'd finally decided to say something, finally decided on what to do about the issue, Alex was gone—killed along the north shore of Lake Winnipeg by a wendigo, they'd said.

He sat facing into the low sun, the driver's door open and letting in the wind. Alex had a lot of explaining to do, but Wilson already knew the answer long before the question was asked. It would be what he'd say were the situation reversed: "I was on a mission. I couldn't." As if being on a mission excused everything. The sad part was that it *did* explain everything, but it still wasn't enough. *Was it ever?* He allowed himself a moment to indulgently sulk.

Rehydrated and steady on his feet, Wilson retrieved his last bit of dirt and placed it into the same sigil-etched silver container that held the other samples. His task was to collect soil from the center of Australia, and he would deliver, Alex or not.

Wilson was thirty miles south of Alice Springs when his phone rang again. His caller ID showed David LaSalle, Leader's primary assistant. He hurriedly pulled onto the shoulder, turned on his hazards, and answered, "This is Fulcrum."

"Fulcrum, I'm calling to inform you that Stigma has returned to the Mine." Each syllable was delivered in LaSalle's precisely enunciated tenor. Wilson had originally thought it an affectation, but every time he'd ever spoken with him, his diction was perfect and his tone melodious.

"I know," Wilson said simply.

"I see. He's spent the past few days recuperating in the Mine and has determined it's unsuitable. He needs a place to stay while he finishes healing, and it needs to be somewhere invisible to any Ivory Tower scrying. As you two worked closely together, I've been asked to see if the 500 is available."

Wilson's brain focused on "recuperating"—*How did Moncrief forget to tell me Alex was injured?*—and it took him a second to process the other words. "No," he answered emphatically. "Under no circumstances should anyone ever attempt to enter the 500 without me being there. To be clear— do not attempt entry. Ever."

"Understood," LaSalle responded professionally.

He was about to follow up, but Wilson interrupted, "Asked by whom?"

"Leader," LaSalle replied.

"I see." Wilson paused before continuing, "My Corktown house could be available if Lancer has no objections," he offered. "There are several spare rooms, and if she's been maintaining the wards, it should be impervious to scrying."

"I'll contact her. LaSalle out."

Wilson tossed the phone onto the passenger seat, checked his mirrors, and reentered the road.

Chapter Eight

Moscow, Russia
17th of August, 8:28 a.m. (GMT+3)

Alexander Petrovich Lukin's coffee had gone cold. He drew back the white polystyrene cup from his lips and placed it on the long snakewood table. Once a truly impressive piece of furniture, decades of self-important apparatchiks demonstrating their personal power by eschewing the use of coasters had revealed that it was only a veneer over a larch wood frame. *Like much of the Communist era*, he thought. *Not that things are better now, he admitted. We're still using the same table, but now we're not even bothering to dress it up with a nice cover.*

He was in a black mood; the past seven days had been rough, starting with an emergency Saturday meeting regarding a mass killing at Club NB, a premier Moscow dance club. More than two hundred had died from some magical source, and the cadre of Ivory Tower imps had no clue who the culprit was except that it was old, devoured souls through mirrors, and definitely wasn't a devil. Worse, a live-streaming video had inadvertently captured the attack. The content was eventually taken offline, but not before millions had already viewed it.

Never one to waste a crisis, it was officially labeled a Chechen terrorist gas attack and condemned in the strongest terms.

While that pot cooled to a simmer, another had boiled over: the *Yantar* went missing five days ago. Once the wreckage was found, teams of divers had confirmed the worst. As the preeminent sea vessel in Russian intelligence, it was an unexpected blow that sent ripples through the entire intelligence community. Who had the capability or the balls to sink the *Yantar*?

Truth be told, Lukin wasn't sure why he was summoned, but here he was, waiting outside the chairman's office for yet another Saturday meeting. He hated Saturday meetings. He dragged his hand through his graying blond hair and rose from the table to refresh his coffee, eyeing the last of the sweet rolls that were only slightly less stale than the air in the room—by the smell of it, it had been a long night.

The door to Chairman Vladimir Volsky's office opened and his personal assistant ushered in the expectant agent. "Sasha Lukin to see you," he announced before shutting them in the room.

"Agent Lukin," the portly man behind the desk stood officiously and greeted him. "Please, sit." Lukin performed a quick scan of the chairman and the room. Volsky's clothes were fresh and his face shaven, but his tired eyes betrayed the long nights spent at work. A thick haze hung in the room, as the chairman was an avid smoker—more so in a crisis—and even though the ashtray was empty, the discarded containers in the wastebasket informed Lukin it had been a four-box night.

Much like the table out front, Volsky was a relic of times past. When the political upheavals of the past thirty years had jostled all other aspects of Russian governance, the Ivory Tower's obscure operation and effective mission rate shielded it from such turmoil. Not that it was above pettiness and personal vendettas—they just kept it in-house.

"Chairman Volsky," he returned the salutation with a firm handshake before taking the proffered seat. "How may I be of service?"

"One week ago, we received a blackout request from Andrei Vasilovich Zarubin, one of our agents stationed at Nemo Sea Laboratory, west of Sal Island in Cape Verde," Volsky began, lighting another cigarette newly liberated from a fresh pack. Lukin's interest piqued; blackouts were a last resort, reserved for when high magical risk warranted overriding original mission parameters. In all his years of service, he had only requested a blackout twice. His grim nod to the chairman indicated he understood the severity of the situation.

The chairman continued, "We have confirmation that our agent rendezvoused with the *Yantar* five nights ago and they were headed to Dakar. Unfortunately, it was sunk before it made it to port, and we were unable to fully debrief our agent. We do not know the nature of the blackout or what Zarubin took with him when he left the Nemo. Early analysis of the wreck suggests the *Yantar* was twisted and wrung out, like a damp dishtowel. We haven't found any survivors nor recovered any bodies from the scene. Zarubin is presumed dead."

He paused and drew deeply on the cigarette; the exhaled smoke hung between them. Volsky knew Lukin to be a keen and perceptive man; he didn't need to explicitly state the suspicious nature and timing of the *Yantar*'s sinking. "Your mission is to uncover the nature of the blackout; whatever it was, Zarubin felt complete destruction of the lab was necessary. More importantly, make sure the risk has been eradicated; the downing of the *Yantar* is less than reassuring and adds to the tally, indicating that the blackout was properly called."

Volsky pulled a slim folder from the stack and handed it to Lukin. "There is a relief diving crew leaving this afternoon and I've secured you a seat. Naturally, the deputy chairman has placed the recovery of all advanced equipment and sensitive information as the top priority of the salvage effort, but he has allotted some resources for esoteric investigation. See Mr. Greedigut for a briefing on Zarubin and his original mission before you leave."

Lukin had worked with Chairman Volsky long enough to know this sufficed as a dismissal. He gave a perfunctory bow as he left the room and wound his way through to the basement in search of Grizel Greedigut, the longest serving of the Ivory Tower imps.

The Ivory Tower had long used imps, whose low standing

among devils made them easy to coax—or coerce—into being helpful. They were inherently magical beings that scurried on the edges of civil fiendish society and had a knack for picking up tidbits of information that might otherwise be inaccessible to those in the mortal realm. While an individual imp was limited to what it knew, a network of imps could effectively crowdsource what was going on, if a little light on the details. It didn't hurt that imps were clannish by nature, even though they were all eventually related to each other—if one didn't know the answer, perhaps another would.

While they were technically fiends, imps were the least evil of the bunch, at least by devil standards, and they were more likely to be naughty or mischievous than outright villainous. That wasn't to say imps *couldn't* cause significant trouble, but their motivation was less likely sheer malevolence then the more stringently nefarious creatures native to hell. In this way, they were not that unlike fairies, although only idiots would make such a comparison where either of those groups could hear it.

Their lowly status and blasé attitude toward evil made them prime targets for bullying by proper fiends, who could mark imps for destruction for the most minor infraction. That was where the Ivory Tower found its greatest allies. The Interior Council euphemistically offered to "liberate" a marked-for-destruction imp in exchange for service. Should an imp agree to the terms, they were bound by the neck with an ivory collar which gave them sanctuary inside the Ivory Tower's complexes. The collars also allowed them to be tracked or—under breach of contract—destroyed. Superficially, it appeared as continued servitude with a change in masters, but from the imps' perspective, the Russians were generally less difficult to work for than devils and the food and entertainment were better in the mortal realm.

Lukin went to the basement, rounded several corners, and found his quarry in his quarters-slash-office. The twelve-inch-tall demon kept his horns short and his beard long, in part to cover his overly rotund belly. It was hard to say which Greedigut loved more: his food, his pipe, or his porn. He was never far from any of them. Based on the moans sounding out of the imp's console, Lukin made an educated guess which was occupying him this morning.

"Griz, you down here?" he called out from the exterior, giving the imp plenty of warning to wrap up whatever he was watching.

"Sasha! What are you doing here?" Greedigut hollered in a voice that was entirely too deep to come from such a small creature. "It's not like you to show up at work on the weekend." The imp turned down the volume but not the video; he had no shame, but did it for the benefit of the human entering the room.

"I'm here for a data dump," Lukin answered him, and found his blue eyes wandering to the screen in spite of himself;

Griz was into some sick shit.

Greedigut sighed at the slight disgust on Lukin's face and the picture went blank. "You really know how to kill a guy's boner." He laughed before shifting gears to focus on work. "What do you need?"

"Background information and objective for the last mission of Andrei Vasilovich Zarubin," Lukin replied.

A faraway look came over the imp's face as he searched his mind. "Got it. How you wanna do this?" he asked.

"The fast way—I've got a flight to catch," Lukin responded emphatically.

"Really?!" Greedigut exclaimed; he knew Lukin's aversion to direct neural transmission. "Okay, but don't fight me—it will only make it harder on both of us," he warned.

The Ivory Tower inadvertently went green when it started using imps for recordkeeping instead of leaving a paper trail that could be traced or stolen. The younger generation of agents regularly got caches of information from imps and thought nothing of it, but Lukin still preferred to do things the old-fashioned way. He didn't have anything against Greedigut personally, but his parents had instilled a basic level of caution when it came to working with fiends, even liberated ones.

"I know the drill, Griz. You don't have to tell me every time," Lukin gruffly replied as he took a seat and reflexively cracked his knuckles.

"I'll stop saying it when you stop resisting," the imp

countered and stood on the table to be eye-level with the tall operative. "Now, let me see those baby blues."

Lukin took a deep breath and reined in his will; he opened his eyes and gazed into the pulsating depths of Greedigut's pitch-black orbs. His synapses lit up as the face and facts of Karl Lundqvist flooded his mind, and despite his urge to pull away, Lukin held the connection; premature disengagement would not only give him a splitting headache, it would necessitate a second transmission. He felt a final surge that tapered off into nothing before he saw Greedigut finally blink. "Was it good for you?" the imp joked.

Lukin blinked a few times. It was over; he had all the information he needed—he just had to think about it, and there would be plenty of time to mull it over on his journey to the waters between Cape Verde and Dakar. He stood up and left the imp to his own devices. "Don't feel bad, Griz. It happens to everyone," he said loudly from the hallway on his way out.

"Sonfabitch!"

Chapter Nine

Detroit, Michigan, USA
17th of August, 6:11 p.m. (GMT-4)

Teresa Maria Martinez flicked her eyes to the wall clock for the third time in ten minutes. She hated waiting, but she got it honestly. Her mother had had an embroidered sampler that had hung in their family home with elaborate scrolls and blooms, along with the text: *Patience is a virtue, and this is proof I have the patience to stab something thousands of times.*

After averting certain death—both personally and world-wide— from the Hollow, Martinez had celebrated in grand fashion last night, first at 18 is 9, and then at a wine bar with Liu and some of her friends. She had glorious plans to do nothing this weekend and catch up on some entertainment binging; her watch list was quickly outpacing her free time.

At least, that had been the plan until LaSalle rang her up and asked if she was amenable to a houseguest—a Salt Mine agent returned from deep cover, who needed somewhere to recuperate that was safe from Ivory Tower scrying. As much as Martinez valued her privacy, she couldn't refuse and knowingly subject someone to live in the Salt Mine when she had a daybed set up in the spare room and a mess of meat marinating in the fridge for the grill. True to form, LaSalle had been short on details, and all he'd given her was an ETA for twenty minutes ago.

She brushed aside the curtain hanging on one of the front windows and peeked out at the street for any sign of her visitor. Her hand ran along the dark oak casing inlayed with ivory sigils, one of the many precautions that came with the house she had slowly come to regard as her space. However, Martinez was under no illusions about why she had been called; Stigma wasn't coming here for her hospitality, only for the security measures Wilson had put in place when he'd lived here.

He should have been here by now, Martinez mulled as she checked the time once more. It wasn't a far drive from Zug Island to Corktown, but it was long enough for an ambush. She had resolved to wait five more minutes before messaging LaSalle when a black Range Rover with factory-tinted windows parked in front of the house. The driver's door opened and LaSalle's towering figure emerged in cargo shorts and a t-shirt, with a casual button-down top thrown over it, just enough to conceal a weapon or two. She had never seen him out of a suit—or out of the Salt Mine, for that matter. She tried to focus on the day-old stubble and ignore the fact that he was wearing socks with his sandals.

He caught Martinez's eye and acknowledged her with a curt nod as he moved to the curbside passenger door. No longer able to observe unseen, she dropped the curtain and walked onto the porch. LaSalle was holding out a pair of crutches for her new guest, who was swiveling out of the seat with his plastered right leg. "Heya!" he called out with a mini-wave before gripping the proffered crutches.

Husnik had dark hair and eyes and his skin was a tawny beige; Martinez couldn't tell if it was genetic or a tan at the height of summer. She had similar issues pinning down his facial features; she'd easily believe him if he said he was Argentinean, Polish, Italian, or from one of the international melting-pot locations like New York.

"Hello!" she greeted the pair, walking down the sidewalk to help with the baggage LaSalle was digging out of the back. "So glad you're here; I was getting worried," she blithely intoned, but LaSalle caught the undercurrent of concern.

"Alex, Teresa; Teresa, Alex," LaSalle gave a hasty introduction. "My apologies for arriving late," he spoke with precision; even though he was out of the suit, he was still using his work voice. "We would have been on time, but he insisted on stopping at a party store." LaSalle handed Martinez two plastic bags filled to the brim with all manner of junk food, including just about every flavor of Slim Jim ever made.

Husnik hobbled out of the car on his good leg and crutches. "All essential kit," he reassured them both. "Wouldn't do to show up unprepared." He returned Martinez's skepticism with an impish wink. He waited until she caught up with him to whisper, "You try getting them when you're in the Russian

Navy."

"I'll keep that in mind before signing up," she responded in Russian.

Husnik's brown eyes lit up in recognition. "Oh, we're going to have fun," he declared as he swung by on his crutches toward the front door.

LaSalle carried the two suitcases to the porch where he deposited them and made his goodbyes—he'd rather never enter the dwelling of another practitioner even if invited. "This is where I leave you two."

"Sure you won't come in for dinner and a beer?" Martinez offered casually. "I was just going to fire up the grill."

LaSalle paused for a millisecond, reading the tone of the invitation. "Maybe some other time," he replied with a warm smile. "You'll have your hands full with this one." His expression turned serious. "And if you have any trouble, just call."

Trouble from Stigma? Trouble from Ivory Tower? Martinez tried to parse his subtext before proverbially throwing up her hands with, *Why not both?* Coming off the heels of the Hollow, Martinez had become very familiar with uncertainty and had adopted a healthy dose of que sera, sera—whatever came up, she'd deal with it. She simply nodded. "Will do. Drive safe!"

Martinez dropped the snacks just inside the door and pulled the luggage inside. Husnik swung his way across the threshold and she closed and locked the door behind them.

"So what's the prognosis on the leg?" Martinez asked as she

brought the foodstuffs into the kitchen.

Husnik paused in the entryway, catching his breath and running his hand along the oak chair rail, like he was greeting an old friend. "They're thinking I'm going to be out for eight weeks or so. It hurt like hell when they put it back in alignment, but that's what these are for." He rattled the bottle of prescription painkillers bulging out of his top pocket. His eyes roamed, covering every inch of the space he once knew so well. The decor was different, and the smells from the kitchen were divine. *David was never one to bother turning sustenance into cuisine*, Husnik mused.

"The guest bedroom is upstairs. Are the stairs doable?" Martinez inquired as she returned from the kitchen.

"Yep, no problem. Just have to take it slowly," he replied. "And thanks for putting me up. Staying in the Mine was…" he searched for the right euphemism.

Martinez stopped him short. "I understand. I inadvertently stayed there overnight during my interview, and one night was enough for me." She motioned toward the living room. "Take a seat and get that leg elevated. I'll just put your things in the spare room." She lugged the two heavy cases slowly up the stairs, mindful not to bang them against the walls.

Husnik crutched over to the sofa, propping his broken leg on the sturdy coffee table, but not before putting a throw pillow under his foot; everything ached a bit less. He sunk into the sofa, listening to Martinez's footsteps above and doing the math on when he could take his next pain pill. Suddenly, the hairs on the back of his neck stiffened and he knew he wasn't alone. He straightened up and looked over his shoulder into the corner of the room and saw friendly figures.

"Ah, Millie, Wolfhard—so nice to see you again!" he exclaimed. He instinctively held up his arms for a hug before he remembered they couldn't embrace, and he played it off as part of his enthusiasm. "Hey little one, how have you been?" he addressed the small ghost playfully peeking out from behind them.

"Alex, we thought you were dead!" Millie blurted out as she rushed to give him an ethereal embrace. Although there was no contact, he felt the outpouring of emotion nonetheless. "Mr. Wilson's going to be so thrilled!"

"Well, we'll see about that," Husnik hedged.

Martinez deftly avoided the creak on the penultimate top step—she didn't want to interrupt the reunion—and noted *Alex* was on a first-name basis with the ghosts but it was still *Mr. Wilson* for Fulcrum. "I see you know our guest," Martinez spoke to her ethereal housemates when she reached the bottom of the stairs. Although she was nonchalant about it, she was genuinely surprised to find the spirits visible in the living room at such an early time. They tended to stay in the attic until she went to sleep, at which point they liked to roam about the house. Manifesting took a lot of energy, an expenditure compounded exponentially based upon the number of viewers.

"Of course we do, Teresa. He lived here for nearly a year with Mr. Wilson," Millie responded.

"You don't say?" she failed to hide her surprise. "I guess that means we can skip the tour and get straight to dinner, if you're hungry," she qualified. "I wouldn't want to tear you away from your Slim Jims."

"If you're cooking what smells so good in the kitchen, count me in. Slim Jims are like Twinkies—they'll keep. Probably longer than we will," he joked.

"In that case, I'll heat up the grill. Can I get you anything to drink before I start cooking?"

"Just the Yoo-hoo in one of the bags, if you would," he requested.

Martinez went to the backyard and turned on the propane-fueled unit before fetching her guest's beverage. She dug out the chocolate drink from one of the overstuffed bags and poured herself an iced tea. She overheard Mille ask the questions one might expect to field when everyone thought you were dead for the past five years: Where have you been? What were you doing? How did you break your leg? Husnik did his best to politely dodge her questions until Wolfhard interceded on his behalf. "Millie, you know he can't talk about work anymore than Mr. Wilson or Teresa can." Martinez smiled—it was a nice reminder that death didn't stop people from being themselves.

Chastised, Mille rephrased her request, "Well, what can you tell us?"

"How about a story?" he offered, and even the quiet one perked up at the suggestion.

"The grill is warming up but it will take a few minutes," Martinez announced as she entered the room and handed Husnik his bottle.

"You're in for a real treat, Teresa," Millie informed her. "Alex is the best storyteller this side of 1900." Wolfhard's terse nod confirmed his wife's declaration to be the truth.

"I love a good story," she answered innocently and took a seat on the chair opposite the couch.

Husnik caught the amusement in Martinez's eyes and nodded appreciatively for the drink and the diversion. He spun his tale of two knights of Camelot who, during their search for the Holy Grail, were forced to stop at a castle for shelter. Unbeknownst to them, the lord of the castle was a foul knight in league with the devil, and he poisoned the knights during the dinner feast. The knights, being pure of heart, refused to surrender to treachery and returned as ghosts. They proved so terrifying that they drove the evil lord out of his castle and over a nearby cliff.

Martinez listened intently, picking up hints of his personality from his vocabulary, inflections, and spoken quirks. Besides having showmanship and flare in the telling, she also gave him credit for picking a story where the heroes were ghosts—he knew how to play to the crowd. It wasn't a long yarn, perhaps ten minutes, and by the end the ghosts were flickering from their long materialization. The harrowing conclusion brought a round of applause before the bulk of the audience excused themselves and faded away to nothing.

"That was quite good," Martinez admitted. Husnik doffed an imaginary hat as he downed the last of his Yoo-hoo. "Not a typical skill for a Salt Mine agent," she observed.

"When I was a kid, the career aptitude tests placed me as a circus barker or a supernatural spy," he drily remarked.

"You may have missed your calling," Martinez feigned misgiving. "Although, how many circuses could there have been in Canada?" She wagered a guess after a bit of Canadian inflection peeked out of his otherwise unaccented English.

Husnik flashed a big smile that made Martinez wonder if the slip was accidental or intentional. "You've got a good ear. Most people can't tell where I'm from. My mom was Canadian, but I spent every summer with my grandparents in Pennsylvania and most of my adult life in the States, when I wasn't pretending to be Russian, of course."

"As one does," she answered his set up. "If it makes you feel better, it wasn't super obvious. It's just that I dated a guy from Alberta and once you hear it, you can't unhear it."

"Did he have a killer mullet and all his teeth, despite playing hockey?" Husnik queried. "Because I may not be the only one who missed their big shot at life fulfillment."

Martinez's full-throated laughter filled the house and reminded Husnik of his own happy times within these walls.

"I'm starving and these ribs aren't going to grill themselves." Martinez rose resolutely with her empty glass. "Wanna keep me company while I cook? Wilson, being Wilson, warded the whole lot, but you can stay inside the house and we can keep the patio door open to be on the safer side."

"Sure." Husnik grabbed the pair of crutches leaning against the side of the sofa. "It's about time for my next pill, and it goes down better with a little food."

Martinez made her way to the kitchen and took stock. "I've got juice and iced tea, and if you need to eat right away, the coleslaw and potato salad are already made. It shouldn't take more than ten minutes for the chicken to cook, maybe twenty for the ribs." She started pulling dishes and flatware from the cabinets and containers from the fridge.

Husnik started salivating when he entered the kitchen and got a better whiff of the marinade. "I'm not judging, but that's an incredible amount of food for just one person." He sounded genuinely concerned.

Martinez laughed. "I cook big when I can so I have homemade food during the times when I can't—I don't need to tell you this job can be a little unpredictable," she wryly understated.

He tapped his cast, "Preaching to the choir," and huffed as he took a seat inside and raised his right leg on another chair.

Martinez tied on her apron and checked the grill; the thermometer said it was ready, and the wave of heat when she opened it confirmed it. She strategically laid the meat out, saving space to grill the zucchini and mushrooms. After she brushed everything down, she took a seat under the awning as it cooked, sipping her iced tea.

"You guessed where I'm from; now it's my turn," Husnik made a game of it. "You sound from the West to these ears."

She applauded him. "Yep. I grew up in California and Colorado."

"Ah! So much nice scenery in both states. Ever been to Sequoia National Park?"

"Is that the one where you can drive through a tree?"

"No, that's the redwoods in Northern California. The sequoias are in Southern California. Both are incredibly beautiful, but the sequoias are my favorite. Go there and then take a trip into the Magh Meall and it will knock your socks off—trees thousands of feet tall. Just unbelievable. An absolute must," he said expansively.

His enthusiasm was infectious, and they chatted about places they'd been and exchanged tips for future vacations. Once all the food was ready, the conversation moved indoors and Martinez was bowled over by all the information that spewed forth. She heard all about his parents' whirlwind romance in the hills and harbor of Dunedin, New Zealand—his mom, a student of international law far from home, and his dad, a Maori engineer that introduced her to his native land. He told her about his blind younger brother, who he had to watch while his mother worked second shift and entertain with his stories during the long summer days at his formerly Amish grandparents' home; they had left the community, but still eschewed certain aspects of modernity and didn't have TV or radio. She noted his use of past tense when speaking of his family but drew no attention to it.

He wasn't sharing for her benefit, but for his own. He hadn't been Alex Husnik for five years; he needed to tell these stories to find his way back, and Martinez was happy to oblige. Even if everything he said turned out to be a lie—he was a spy, after all—at least it was an entertaining rich tapestry. As he wove narratives, she tried to imagine what it must have been like for him and Wilson to inhabit the same house with such different personalities, but she didn't really *know* either of them. That's the problem with their line of work—you only see what they want you to see, and Martinez admitted she wasn't any different.

She changed subjects as she dished out the ice cream, which Husnik immediately covered with Magic Shell, another concoction from his party store run. "So besides the junk food, what have you missed since you've been gone?"

He cracked the top and savored his first bite of dessert. "American TV," he answered after some thought. "Especially the really bad reality shows. They're being exported around the globe, but no one does contrived stupid drama like Americans."

Martinez couldn't argue—she had been known to

indulge from time-to-time. "Well, you'll have your fill while you recuperate. I've got a million channels, and my online streaming accounts are plugged into the TV. That was actually my original plan for this weekend—couch surf and chill."

Husnik recognized the look on her face. "Just finished a big case?"

Martinez acknowledged his perceptive eye and nodded. "It was a rough one, but the world didn't end so I'm counting it as a win."

"Any landing you can walk away from is a good landing," he aphorized.

"It wasn't all bad," she added. "I got an IOU for a getaway with Clover and her sweet ride." Martinez carefully crafted a bite that was mostly vanilla ice cream with a little banana and nuts.

"Don't you love her jet?!" he gasped. "It's much nicer than the one she had before I died, and I didn't think that was possible."

"How did she take your resurrection?" Martinez probed gently.

"She squealed and hugged me. Then punched me hard. Then hugged me harder," he recounted.

Martinez giggled and swallowed her sweet treat. "You know, if the Salt Mine ever goes tits up, we could always pitch a reality TV show. *Real Agents of the Salt Mine!* Leader could be the one that says 'I'm not here to make friends.'"

Husnik chuckled at the thought. "See? I told you we were going to have fun."

Chapter Ten

Spasatel Zaborschikov, Sal Island, Cape Verde
19th of August, 9:19 a.m. (GMT-1)

Lukin hated helicopters. He hated the noise. He hated the way they had to roll forward to move forward and roll backward to move backward. He hated how difficult it was to read on his phone while they were in the air, and consequently he couldn't distract himself from the fact he was a thousand feet above the water, held up by nothing but an oversized fan. Most of all, he hated that they crashed more often than planes, and they tended to do their crashing on take-offs and landings.

This was at the forefront of his mind as the Ka-226 dropped toward the deck of the *Zaborschikov*. He tapped his hand nervously against the briefcase containing his gear, which included his phone containing recordings of the video feed from the remotely operated vehicles currently scouring the wreck of the *Yantar*. Some things couldn't be neural-uploaded.

The transition between hovering and landing seemed to take forever, and he thought they would never reach the deck, until he finally felt the familiar bump of touchdown. Lukin immediately relaxed and gladly exited the noisy machine for the safety of the ship's superstructure. His arrival caused a stir of activity and speculation among the crew—the passenger must be someone important to warrant an unscheduled drop.

Pavel Smolin, captain of *Zaborschikov*, knew better. He didn't exactly understand why Commander Alexander Petrovich Lukin was necessary, only that someone higher up called in a "specialist" to look for something in particular among the wreckage.

Specialist—the term stuck in Smolin's craw; so non-descript as to tell you nothing, but still precise enough to adequately convey superiority. Wasn't his crew more than equipped and capable of carrying out the salvage of the *Yantar*, spy ship or not? But it was not his place to ask, even if Lukin's presence was an implicit questioning of his judgment. He had been given orders, and he would follow them, even when they irked him.

Smolin was there to greet Lukin on deck, but he did not bother to hide his displeasure. He may have to treat Lukin's requests as orders, but he certainly didn't have to kiss his ass. Lukin, on the other hand, had little time to waste on petulant captains and brushed off the tepid reception. Instead, he requested a private space and a large monitor into which he could plug in his phone. He had hours more of footage to watch before he was up to date regarding the salvage operation. Once he'd caught up, he'd join the crew in the observation room for the real-time feed.

He fortified himself with a cup of coffee and some bread and butter while the crew accommodated him, and within no time, he was holed up in his own nook of the *Zaborschikov*. Lukin started scanning the video of the salvage up to now, hoping to find out more than he already deciphered—the *Yantar* had been ripped in half, and whatever had done it wasn't mundane. Hour after hour of tedium passed until his stomach and his brain came to an agreement—it was time for food.

Lukin requested the recordings from the past two days on his way to the commissary. If he timed everything correctly, he could get through all of the video footage and still catch a few hours of sleep tonight before starting with the live feed in the morning. He happily gulped down his *makarony po-flotsky* amid the banal pleasantries in the mess, and got back to work as quickly as he could, another coffee in hand.

Zaborschikov had three remotely operated vehicles. The largest was nearly large enough for a man to fit within if needed; the next largest was about man-sized, and the final wasn't must larger than a hefty suitcase. To speed things up, Lukin multi-screened the three feeds instead of reviewing them serially. It required more attentiveness, but time was of the essence.

Lukin paused the recording when something of potential interest popped up on the smallest ROV's feed. It was working its way through the crew quarters, and its standard operating procedure was to enter a chamber, pan around, exit, and move on to the next room. Amid the debris, a flash of orange peeked out of a storage locker. It looked like fabric, but standard issue naval duffle bags weren't orange.

Lukin rewatched the footage and weighed his options. He knew he essentially had complete command of the ship, but he didn't want to rub Captain Smolin's face in it. He didn't know how long he would be aboard, and burning social capital this early on would be unwise. It took a few more viewings before he decided the cloth was intriguing enough to investigate immediately. He had to speak to Captain Smolin and commandeer the smallest ROV.

Lukin found him in the control center. Smolin wasn't happy with the idea—it would mean moving the rover a significant distance to cover ground they had already surveyed—but he backed Lukin, who'd had the foresight to frame it as a request, not an order.

"Do as Commander Lukin suggests, Yakovlev," Captain Smolin instructed his man.

"Yes, sir!" the petty officer third class responded.

Lukin watched as the young officer guided the smallest of the ROVs out of the engine room and into the crew quarters. It took some time, as the ROV didn't move quickly and the current was strong where the ship was twisted in two. Eventually the vehicle threaded its way back to the starboard side quarters.

"There!" Lukin said when the flash of orange appeared on the screen.

"Grab that object, Petty Officer, and bring it to the surface," Smolin ordered.

Yakovlev deftly maneuvered the ROV until the fabric caught

in its claw. He shifted the ROV into reverse, but it struggled as it backed up—the object was caught against something. The petty officer worked quickly and turned the ROV around to pull from the other direction. He released his held breath when an orange bag slid freely out of the storage locker. Thick black letters were stamped on its side: Skliar, Myroslav.

"That's the Ukrainian terrorist's!" Captain Smolin exclaimed.

Lukin nodded. "I need to see what's in there, immediately. Can you bring it up to the surface intact?" In his excitement, he dropped all pretense that Captain Smolin was in charge.

"It will take some time, but I think I can find a clear path, sir," Yakovlev replied.

"I'll be aft waiting," Lukin said as he left the ROV recovery area.

"I'll join you," Captain Smolin added. "Good work, Yakovlev."

*****

The sailors on deck went to work once the little ROV breached the surface, dragging a large orange bag in its claw. They latched the crane onto its hardpoint with a specially designed gaff and the ROV was on the deck of *Zaborschikov* within minutes. Once the ROV released the bag from its claw, Captain Smolin turned it to drain as much of the water out as he could, an ample demonstration of the difference between water resistant and waterproof.

Lukin stayed Smolin's enthusiasm with a sober, "Away from the crew?"

Smolin nodded. "This way," he said under his breath. He led Lukin to the nearby ROV storage room and ordered the sailors there to leave. Lukin closed the door behind them and indicated to the captain that he would like to have the bag. Smolin was acutely aware that Lukin was between him and the only exit, and acquiesced.

Lukin set the bag on the floor before threading out his will and examining it for magical dangers. As he did so, the captain waited, unsure what his unwanted visitor was doing. Why was he just staring at it?

When Lukin detected nothing on his cursory pass, he carefully unzipped the bag. Within was a collection of clothing, which he examined piece by piece. Each was consistent with Zarubin's cover story and none were of interest. He was about halfway through the bundle when a thin waterlogged book and a small tin box shaped like a steamer trunk covered in vintage stamps fell out of the pile of clothing.

Lukin threaded out his will again, checking for charms, wards, explosives, and elemental magic on the box. Again, it was clear. When Lukin popped it open, the trap Zarubin had put in place—the one to ensure he'd know who'd been messing with his stuff—went off. It was a simple magic, so elementary that Lukin hadn't thought to check for it. It was the kind of trap that children would use in boarding school: a stink bomb, one that only magically sensitive creatures could smell.

Lukin cursed as the rank odor washed over him. *Zhizn' ebet meya! How could I have been so stupid!* He'd stink like a dead fish until he could get back to the Ivory Tower and perform the cleansing ritual; dried skunk glands weren't for purchase at local markets.

"Something wrong?" Smolin asked, surprised by the vehemence of Lukin's reaction to a tin filled with damp cards, a multi-tool, and what looked like bits of clockwork.

"Just angry," Lukin brushed him off. "Angry that there's nothing here. I thought we'd found something."

Smolin smiled over Lukin's shoulder, taking pleasure in his frustration. "Such is the way of this business," he lamented out loud while laughing internally. *Such a specialist!*

Chapter Eleven

Wilson had flown in hundreds of planes since starting his career, first in the CIA and then for the Salt Mine. While large commercial flights relied on the power and speed of jets, he still favored the gentle hum and rumble of propeller craft over the explosive roar that pushed against his gut. He looked out the window of the ATR 72 Turboprop as it soared over the sea on its approach toward Sal Island.

Wilson had anticipated a change in plans once he'd heard of Alex's return, and his suspicions had come to fruition. The day before he was supposed to fly out of Australia for Detroit, the Salt Mine had sent word for him to investigate the destruction of the Nemo Sea Laboratory and—if he could get close and dive deep enough—the *Yantar*. He wasn't the only agent qualified in scuba, but he was the most experienced and the only one with a completely free schedule.

Unlike the previous request to stop by the Solomon Islands, this was only cutting into his return trip and jetlag recovery, a fair trade-off considering he got to do more diving while getting part of his vacation paid for. He also had the benefit of getting the real story behind the spin, devouring the briefing as soon as it arrived on his phone. It had laid it all bare: the destruction of the Nemo by an Ivory Tower agent and the sinking of the *Yantar* at the hands of water elementals.

Wilson found this shocking—the *Yantar* had been small by modern military standards, but it was in a whole different class of sea vessel than the fishing boats previously attacked. On paper, it shouldn't be possible to get that many water elementals to work together. Wilson considered himself a passable magician and he'd worry about getting more than two or three to coordinate their efforts, much less enough to crack open a ship the length of a football field. *Another occurrence to add to the file of magic that isn't functioning as it is supposed to.* The report posed two worrisome questions: who was controlling the elementals and just how big of a ship could they take down?

Wilson had read over Stigma's debriefing five times, not wanting to miss a single detail. Alex had always had a way with words; even his official reports contained a streak of the storyteller. Although Wilson hadn't been told as such, and the report didn't directly address it, he had no doubt that the analysts were taking apart all the information on the recovered memory stick, and that Martinez had taken Alex in at the Corktown house. In the quiet moments between bouts of concentration, Wilson had wondered what five years in the Russian navy looked like on him.

Wilson pondered the thought once more as the turboprop

descended for its landing. The barren, sandy brown landscape the plane dropped into was a far cry from the lush green of the Solomon Islands, but Wilson knew from experience that an entirely new world opened up once he entered the great blue of the sea. He found it hard to believe they were entering the "wet season"—most of the rain came in August and September—but what could be expected from a place that received less than twelve inches of rain annually? The plants were sparse and tan, and those that weren't were prickly and tough, or so deep-rooted they could weather the inhospitable climate.

The plane landed with unusual grace and Wilson retrieved his luggage and scuba gear from baggage claim, loaded it into the back of his rented Suzuki Jimny, and drove a brief few miles west to Palmeira, where his hotel waited, along with local boat rentals. He had direct instructions to make the captain of whichever boat he rented pliable for whatever the mission needed. It was rare for Leader to venture a tactical opinion in a brief, and he took that as an indication of how seriously she was taking the matter.

The hotel wasn't anything special, but the reservation was for the top floor corner looking out over the water. Wilson smiled when he got to the balcony during his initial walk-through of the room. It was a perfect vantage point. Once he'd settled in, he retrieved his compact 12x50 binoculars, sat down to brace his arms against shake, and looked out to sea at his objectives.

Wilson had two wreck sites to visit for this mission. The first site, the one over the Nemo Lab, was empty and should prove easy. The second, however, was going to be difficult…if not impossible. The water over the *Yantar* site was populated by a large military vessel that he assumed was Russian—it had a flag, but the wind was blowing such that he couldn't see it— and two smaller craft which he assumed were associated with the larger vessel. A second vessel flying the Cape Verde flag was nearby. It was significantly smaller than the Russian ship and had the looks of a Cape Verde coast guard patrol boat.

He observed the site for a half hour to confirm his initial assessment. *Well, that location's off the list*, he thought. He wouldn't be able to infiltrate it unobserved, and he didn't have a cover that would allow him to do it under the pretense of official approval. He then turned his binoculars to Palmeira Harbor.

The analysts at the Salt Mine had provided a list of three possible captains to target for his needs. Each was considered bribable enough for Wilson to approach backed up with some mild charming. He needed a captain to take him to the Nemo site and remain over it while he explored the wreckage, but he couldn't just magically charm his way there like a bull in a coffee shop, because he needed a captain that could adequately judge the risks of the sea while Wilson was underwater.

Charming—at least when performed by human magicians—turned the target into an automaton if used too heavily. Most of the time it wasn't an issue, as agents usually needed simple things, but it did mean that the deeper skills the mark possessed weren't available to the charmer since the charm temporarily erased the free will necessary to make good decisions based upon education and intelligence. It was easy to use magic to get someone to open a door for you; it was impossible to charm someone to give you their professional opinion of a complex situation.

Wilson ran his binoculars over the harbor, looking for the three boats. Within a few seconds he'd located one, and in a few more he found a second. He carefully looked over each of the vessels to determine which was the shabbiest and decided upon one. Wilson discounted the third vessel entirely, as its absence at the dock at this time of day suggested it was out doing *something* earning money. For his purposes, the more financial leverage, the better. He watched for about a half hour until he saw someone board the vessel he'd targeted—the *Fortuna*.

*****

The captain of the *Fortuna* was Tito Gabriel Lopes da Silva. He was bandy-legged, rough-handed, and a few drinks farther along than Wilson preferred. He was also easily talked into a night dive in exchange for ten crisp one hundred dollar bills in an unsealed white envelope. Wilson didn't even have to charm him, and he found Mr. Silva's complete lack of interest in his affairs refreshingly honest: Silva was a man who could be bought and he knew it. In fact, he wished it would happen more often than it did.

In the dead of night, Wilson boarded the *Fortuna*. It was much like its captain—sketchy but surprising reliable, all things considered. For all its run-ins, it had seen better days, but the engine ran well and the hull was good. They ran without lights, and the black waves smoothly rolled along its side as it carried Wilson to the waters above the destroyed Nemo lab. Silva killed the engine and nodded before whispering, "We're here."

Wilson had kitted out on the short ride and quickly dropped into the ebony water. He stayed on the surface for a brief moment, adjusting all of his gear—he'd come loaded for bear. It was unlikely that there would be water elementals in or around the lab, but he didn't take chances. He had two three-liter jugs filled with concentrated vinegar dyed red, one in case he met an elemental and the second to cover his return to the *Fortuna*.

Once he had secured everything to him, Wilson turned his body and swam downward. After he had put some distance between himself and the surface, he switched on his primary light. It was a strong, wide beam, and he wanted to ensure nothing would reach the surface. The primary fixture attached to a head mount that allowed him full use of his hands, and his backup lights were arm-mounted.

As he descended, Wilson found the growing pressure comforting, like a weighty blanket on a cold night. He was halfway down when the remains of the Nemo Lab came into view, and he could immediately tell it was a deliberate scuttling. Based on the breakage and pattern of debris, at least four charges had been set, if not more.

Wilson mentally reconstructed the structure so it matched the schematics in the briefing documents and identified his first target: the private sector lab. If something unusual had been taking place on the Nemo, it would probably be there, rather than in the research facilities shared by the cadre of international scientists.

He did a thorough exterior reconnoiter before entering. It should have been safe, considering the Cape Verde coast guard and police force had already processed the area, and the owner of the laboratory, Karl Lundqvist, had already removed anything of value. But Wilson was cautious by nature and not pressed for time.

As he swam the length of the converted Whisky-class submarines, he noted their hulls were intact and the water must had entered in via the connecting superstructure of the lab—consistent with his brief and initial observations. It also meant he had no external exits through the hull once he was inside. He pushed his will ahead of him—*think, think, think*—lightly probing the surroundings for any sign of magical warding.

Content that there weren't any exterior dangers, Wilson

carefully avoided the sharp metal edges of one of the explosion zones and slipped into the lab via the closest hole. The interior was a mess, and he slowly swam down a metallic corridor to the entrance of the converted submarine, taking extra care to avoid debris. Wilson had a moment of concern when he saw the hatch to the converted submarine was closed—had the Lundqvist salvage party sealed it shut when they left? He breathed a sigh of relief when it opened with a bit of effort.

He checked again for magical wards, and this time he found three: one against scrying, one against faeries, and one against devils. Wilson took note; whatever Lundqvist or his associates were doing in the submarine, they didn't want to be bothered, enough to take basic precautions.

Wilson probed for a few more minutes to make sure he hadn't missed anything before entering the flooded hull of the old Whisky-class submarine. The first thing he noticed was that it was better apportioned than the communal areas of the lab. The furnishings, although restricted by the spatial limitations, were superior in every way. The second thing he noticed was the current.

Wilson grabbed onto a pipe as a sinking feeling came over him. Everything that could be flooded should be by now, and with the exterior of the hull sealed and intact, the only interior access was the one he'd just come through. There shouldn't be a current unless he had company.

Cautiously, he returned to the hatch and the corridor

beyond until he found what he was looking for: a piece of debris large enough to wedge open the hatch. If he didn't want to be trapped in a steel vessel with an angry water elemental, he had to ensure it had a place to flee. Once secured, he returned to the submarine, this time with a jug of vinegar ready to deploy. He slowly crept forward, and when he felt the current again, he switched on both of his backup lights.

Seeing a water elemental underwater was daunting task, but with multiple light sources, his chances of seeing the ripples of a water elemental's body improved. It would look like heat waves rising from a hot road, only mobile and aggressive.

The current led him toward the front of the submarine and the watery metal corridor channeling down the entire length of the vessel. Even with his precautions, he didn't see the elemental until it was nearly upon him. He popped the top of the vinegar bottle in his hand and the red liquid rapidly gushed out due to the pressure differential between the interior of the bottle and the surrounding seawater.

The water elemental made contact and slammed Wilson against the steel wall of the central corridor. It felt like being hit by a freight train. His vision tunneled and he realized his mask had been knocked off kilter as he grunted in pain. Just as he was about to lose consciousness, the shark-tooth choker around his neck flashed a deep lilac and a bubble of air magically surrounded his head.

Wilson returned to full consciousness a second later and

spun his head around, looking for the elemental. Fortunately, it was nowhere to be seen, and given the rose tint of the water and its direction of flow, the elemental had retreated out the open hatch. He secured his gear, double-checking that nothing had been damaged and that the air from his dislodged mask was flowing as expected. Then, he lowered the spell on his necklace by saying, "Thank you, Little Mother, for sparing the life of your faithful servant."

The necklace had been a gift from a shaman he'd helped in Halmahera on one of his first international missions. It contained the spirit of her great-grandmother. He'd been warned to only use it when absolutely necessary, as the shaman's great-grandmother had a short temper and was slowly escaping her binding. Eventually she'd find her way out, and the necklace would cease to work. This was only the second time he'd used it; the first was a test in controlled conditions to make sure it actually worked.

Using the various protrusions on the wall, he ever so slowly pulled himself toward the front of the submarine. He didn't want to disturb the vinegar "plug" in the corridor, as it was an effective water-elemental deterrent. Leaving all his lights on, he crawled along in this fashion for a good ten feet before he paused to see if he could feel any more currents. Once he was certain the water was still, he resumed swimming.

It didn't take long to reach the end of the corridor, and he threaded out his will once more to check for any additional guards or wards around the final bulkhead. With the rose-vinegar haze undisturbed behind him and the water clear ahead of him, he entered the large bow chamber, but he was not expecting what was on the other side.

Unlike the rest of the submarine, the bow chamber had been heavily modified. Everything was toppled out of place from the force of the rushing water as it had flooded the chamber, but there were all the remains of a well-apportioned living room inside—a significant transformation for the room that had once held the submarine's massive torpedoes and their impressive firing mechanisms.

He checked his air supply to see how much time he had to search before inspecting the large room. While all the furniture was large, all the pieces were sectional. The large L-shaped couch could be divided into individual seats, and the queen-sized bed separated into two smaller mattresses. Everything could be rendered small enough to fit through the central corridor and the restrictive exterior hatch.

Wilson swam around for ten minutes, inspecting nooks and crannies, cabinets and jostled bookshelves—looking for any hint at what warranted a guard, even after the Nemo was scuttled. Despite his best efforts, it alluded him. He went over the room again, this time even slower, and still nothing caught his eye. Frustrated, he checked down the corridor and saw the rose color rapidly diffusing.

Running out of time, Wilson closed his eyes and mentally

reset. It was a tactic he'd learned from the CIA—to reapproach something with a clean slate, close your eyes and when you open them, see what is off. One of the wag recruits had called it "the world's most dangerous game of 'Spot the Difference.'"

He opened his eyes and the first thing he saw was that everything was sectional…everything except the brass table solidly wedged between the couch and two chairs. Wilson knew it when he saw it—that was entirely too big to fit through the hatch. Dislodging it took some effort, but he eventually freed it. It was a square table that he eyeballed as nearly six feet per side. *I should have seen it earlier*, he chided himself. *Sometimes it's the obvious things that you miss.*

Upon closer inspection, Wilson thought it was gunmetal—red brass—which was highly resistant to corrosion from steam and salt water. He tried to move it, but decided against it once he realized how heavy it was—at least three hundred pounds. He ran his fingers over the top, trying to see if he could detect anything. The thick slab of metal was smooth and polished, held up by a metal frame not unlike what you would find with glass-topped tables.

He gave one of his rare smiles when he it dawned on him that there were two sides to the tabletop. He flipped over and swam along the floor of the submarine until he could see the other side.

Bingo!

Etched into the underside was a series of three circles, one large and two smaller. The small circles were connected to the larger circle via a line, and the arrangement reminded him of the structure of a water molecule. Along the circumference of the circles was writing. Wilson edged closer so he could read the text, and it was only then he realized what he was looking at.

It was an attunement circle.

Crap.

Chapter Twelve

Karl Lundqvist stood on the prow of his yacht, anchored for the night off the West African coast. The twinkling lights of the shore were a mere extension of the dark starry night. Tomorrow he would fly back to Monaco with the Nemo Sea Lab behind him, literally and metaphorically.

When he first heard of the explosion, he'd assumed it was a horrific accident, but once he'd found out about the sunken Russian ship he grew suspicious. It was certainly plausible that Skliar blew up the *Yantar* in a ruse of being stranded at sea, but Lundqvist couldn't imagine what the Ukrainian had against him or the other scientists at the lab. Could a man of science be so determined to strike a blow to the country that annexed his home that he would blow up such an edifice to his discipline?

The Swede couldn't say with any certainly, but he knew there was another possibility regarding the sinking of the *Yantar*. He worried it was his fault. His last command to the elementals had been to protect the lab and his section of the sea cable. He knew in the past they'd attacked fishing boats that got too close, but the damage to the *Yantar* was on another scale. The fishing boats had just been disabled or driven off, not sunk. He hadn't imagined his watery servants capable of such destruction, but he was honest enough with himself to know that he wasn't exactly a virtuoso when it came to magic. And it wasn't the sort of thing he wanted to discuss with Hans, his brother, who was.

Regardless of the reason for the sinking of the Russian ship, Lundqvist knew the area was too hot to continue operations. He'd arrived in the waters of Cape Verde as soon as he'd heard, under the pretense of personally wanting to oversee the cleanup of his underwater laboratory. With his hired crew working to the east and the Russians camped over the remains of their vessel to the north, *The Duchess* had slipped in without incident. As a seasoned diver, no one batted an eye when the Swede and two bodyguards had suited up and entered the water to retrieve items. He had breathed a sigh of relief once he'd secured the device from the sea cable.

Now that he was so close to a safe retreat, he allowed himself time to mourn the loss of what he considered his greatest legacy to oceanography. The inconvenience to his business was incidental—largely because it could be made up in other areas—however, the Nemo had been unique.

Lundqvist had always loved being in the water. He loved the feel, the sheer physical embrace, and he loved the philosophical experience of malleable perspective and orientation while under water. As a teen, he'd escaped his cold and dreary Sweden—

home to his equally cold and dreary family—at every chance, and by the time he was twenty he had dived in every ocean in the world. He was only able to do such because no one in the family took him seriously.

Magnus was the eldest, diametrically different from Karl. Magnus had gone to the right schools, married into the right family, and went into the family business—Lundqvist Investments. Karl had gone wherever was desperate enough to accept him and the sizable institutional donations that came along with him.

Magnus never questioned the professional or social trajectory expected of him, and he had even tried his hand at magic. Not that he was any good at it, but the fact that he made an attempt seemed to please their mother. Karl, on the other hand, couldn't care less. He'd deftly avoided matrimonial arrangements, eschewed business and law school both for the world of programming, and largely regarded magic as an outdated tool in a technological age. Why scry for his misplaced keys when it was faster to use an app and it didn't result in banging one's shin against a table once karma eventually caught up?

If his father had Magnus, his mother had Hans, the only one of her sons with a real aptitude for magic. This left Karl to be whoever he wanted, so he'd poured his innovation and skill in the realm of ones and zeros into his passion: the world's oceans. Karl was researching marine life and habitats, developing emerging technology, crafting equipment for underwater exploration, and bankrolling expeditions to hunt up lost hordes lingering at the bottom of the sea.

After he'd developed and sold his second software company, he'd bought his first yacht and started treasure hunting—not for the money, but for the thrill of discovery. By the time he was thirty, he had three yachts stationed all around the world, one flight away from sailing a different sea at his whim. Since then, his fleet had doubled in size, all decorated with treasures from his dives and nautical memorabilia. The opening of the Nemo Sea Laboratory had been the culmination of a lifelong love of the ocean.

Karl had been happy that he'd gotten out of the expectations placed upon him; freed from his familial albatross, so to say. But everything became muddled when his father died and left him and Magnus to manage the family business. Fortunately for Lundqvist Investments, Karl had a firm grasp on which way the wind was blowing, and he brought the company into the twenty-first century. Magnus fought him at each turn, until one of Karl's programs became the vehicle for immediate electronic inclusion in the New York Stock Exchange. Whatever objections Magnus may have had about his brother's life choices, he had an innate respect for the movement of money and nothing was more sacrosanct to him than the bottom line. With that development, Karl was welcomed back into the family fold and business thrived with a judicious use of Karl's skill and the

Lundqvist family's magical resources.

Karl's introduction into the world of finance and investment gave him a front-row seat to what he'd always been told: the more money one had, the easier it was to make money. It was the only way he could explain how his family had managed to stay in business for so long without modernizing. After all, constantly using magic to prop up a losing proposition was ultimately unsustainable due to the karmic cost. Faced with this reality, Karl had turned it into a game: how much money could he make with as little risk as possible using technology?

It turned out to be a lot. A *lot* of money.

He couldn't remember when in his education that he'd stumbled upon arbitrage, but it was an epiphany. Once he learned everything he could about the subject, he knew he'd found his fiscal calling; by simultaneously buying and selling something on different markets, he could make money off the difference of price at the two places. It didn't matter if it was stocks, currencies, or commodities because he never actually owned or held anything—he made money by moving it around electronically. It was basically legal grifting made possible on a massive scale by electronic trading and precise programming. Sure, the gains per unit were marginal—a percent of a percent of a percent—but when you were trading in a large enough volume, the profits could become astronomical with little to no risk. It was just about timing. Karl had always had good timing.

It was the search for ever-better methods of arbitrage that led him to tapping into the sea cables that crisscrossed the world's oceans. He wanted an unbeatable competitive advantage, and knowing things before everyone else was hard to beat. It was then that a second epiphany came to him: *magical arbitrage*. He finally saw a utility for magic: to use it in situations where the yield was greater than the karmic expense. In that paradigm, there was no risk and only reward. It took considerable resources to set up, not just financially, but magically.

Things were going so well...until they weren't. Until his water elementals were attacking ships. Until someone blew up his Nemo.

Karl's somber gaze lingered on the dark water as he raised his glass one final time in the general direction of the Nemo Sea Lab and said his goodbyes. The gentle rocking of *The Duchess* was interrupted by the shrill tone of Lundqvist's phone, bringing him out of his reverie. He pulled it out of his pocket and checked the caller ID flashing on the screen: Magnus Lundqvist. *How odd*, Karl puzzled as he swiped to answer the call; it wasn't like his brother to phone when he could pass messages via one of his lackeys or text if direct communication was necessary. "Hello, Magnus. To what do I owe the honor of your call?"

A growl preceded any greeting. "Do you always have to be such an ass, Karl?" Magnus slurred slightly, without any attempt to conceal his displeasure.

A broad smile drew across Karl's face; needling his brother was one of his favorite pastimes. He knew he shouldn't indulge, but he made it so easy. "What can I say? Family brings out the best in me." Karl heard the ice clink against the empty glass through the line. *Drunk calling? This just keeps getting better.* "But seriously, is everything all right?"

A terse bitter laugh answered his question. "We have a problem. Our IT department claims we were hacked over the weekend. They don't know the full extent of what was taken, but they have investor information, asset holdings, banking information—"

"Shit," Karl cursed loudly into the night. The clientele of Lundqvist Investments were not the type that took kindly to security breaches, especially when it centered on their money. "Do they know who's behind it?"

"They think it was the Russians."

"You sink our ship, we sink you?" Karl guessed in his worse Russian accent.

"This is no time for jokes," Magnus rebuked him. "You do not want to piss off the Russians."

"Relax. I'm sure it's just a coincidence. Russian hackers are a ubiquitous hazard of doing business online these days. They're like the Nigerian princes of the late 90s. I'm catching a flight out of Dakar tomorrow. I'll head back to the office as soon as I land and see what I can find," Karl reassured his brother; he'd hired the best team but no one knew his code like he did.

"That isn't the worst of it," Magnus's tone darkened. "I've word that the financial news is about to report that Lundqvist Investments has been compromised. Naturally, our investors are on edge." Karl knew an understatement when he heard one.

"No problem. You handle the old guard, I'll charm the young ones, and we'll hide Hans away until this all blows over," Karl affected levity and was rewarded with an honest chuckle—their middle brother was the wiz at magic, but not so much with people and business. "Hold down the fort, and I'll be back as soon as I can."

Chapter Thirteen

Wilson was awake but he kept his eyes closed and his breathing steady nonetheless; he enjoyed the peace and quiet he received when everyone thought he was still asleep. In the past month, he had flown in nearly a dozen planes, but this flight had been by far the most comfortable—he'd even managed to sleep a whole six hours, which was quite the feat for someone who could rarely sleep on planes. He'd zigzagged so many time zones, it was a miracle he wasn't more jet-lagged than he was—just a little tension around the eyes and fuzziness in the brain since his last shot of caffeine had worn off while he slept.

"Rise and shine, sleepy head," Moncrief sung out in a cheerful tone. She drew up the shade covering one of the windows, and bright light spilled into the cabin. "We land in ninety minutes."

Wilson yawned and stretched, wiping the sleep from his eyes. The five-foot-two blonde was still in her pajamas—a two-piece cotton set with little flying pigs soaring through billowing clouds against a blue sky—with her hair pulled back in a ponytail; she looked more like a teenager at a slumber party than a billionaire heiress-slash-covert Salt Mine agent. She sauntered to the seat across from his and tucked her legs under her. Moncrief was always a picture, but it was the glass of fresh-squeezed orange juice in her hand that drew the majority of his attention. "Is that for me?" He nodded at the juice.

Like clockwork, a platter appeared beside him with an identical glass. "Good morning, Mr. Westwood," the steward greeted him. Wilson accepted the drink and nodded at the sound of his current alias's name: Daniel Westwood, private security for Alicia Elspeth Hovdenak Moncrief. "Breakfast will be ready in half an hour," the steward announced before retreating to the dining area.

Moncrief waited until Wilson took a sip of juice and maneuvered his seat from lay-flat to upright before beginning her interrogation. "Sooo…" Moncrief drew out the vowel. "Did you have a chance to see Alex while you were back in Detroit?"

"Alicia, I barely had time to go home, do laundry, and repack for the mission," Wilson deftly avoided answering the question. "As it was, they had to send me the briefing electronically." Leader had everything lined up just so: the "hack" of Lundqvist Investments and subsequent leak to the press was just the excuse Clover needed to get Fulcrum into place for infiltration. She was a major investor in Lundqvist—not just in a personal capacity, but also as a voting board member of numerous organizations. Truth be told, the kudos really belonged to the finesse of the Salt Mine's coders, who used the backdoor on the memory stick that Stigma had recovered and made it look like an honest hack with a subtle Russian calling card.

Moncrief read the room and decided not to pick a fight. "He looks good, except for the broken leg," she remarked offhand. She shrugged her slim shoulders indifferently and tossed her head to the side. "Life at sea agrees with him."

Wilson rose with purpose. "I need to freshen up and review everything one more time before we land," he changed the subject on his way to the bathroom. He had considered stopping by Corktown before leaving to meet Moncrief, but decided against it. Seeing Alex would only distract him; if he didn't see him, he could still pretend Alex was dead until the mission was done. It had been a while since he'd done a cover-backed infiltration, and if everything went according to plan, he might be Daniel Westwood for some time yet. Better to leave David Wilson and all his worries behind.

He methodically performed his ablutions, and in the process started washing away David Wilson and becoming Daniel Westwood. Of all the aliases he had adopted over the years, this one was the closest to Wilson's actual skills and mindset: Westwood was special forces turned private security. He was terse and serious, cautious and calculating, and most importantly, was magically savvy. Wilson enjoyed Westwood, as he didn't have to exert the energy to be socially engaging because that wasn't Westwood's job, and he could reserve that energy for environmental surveillance, situational awareness, and preemptory action.

Adopting an adjacent alias wasn't as hard as a distant one, but it still had its pitfalls if an agent didn't keep clear lines of demarcation between the two personas. It was easy for the real person to slip through when the agent didn't have to try so hard to pretend to be someone else. To keep himself attuned, Wilson focused on the ways he and Westwood differed and deliberately choose the latter until that felt natural. Thus, Daniel Westwood emerged impeccably dressed and ready for breakfast.

He was halfway through his ham and cheese omelet when Moncrief joined him, dressed in a flouncy crêpe sundress with her ponytail transformed into a French twist. She left the matching accessories to the side as well as the short jacket with three-quarter sleeves—perfect for transitioning a stroll along the Riviera into a business meeting. Her blue eyes lit up at the fresh coffee and croissant that awaited her. "Good morning, Westwood," she greeted him as she drew the cloth napkin across her lap.

"Ms. Moncrief," he coolly replied. Westwood wasn't the sort to rise when a lady approached, delay a meal because someone was late, or be on a first-name basis with employers. "I've reviewed the files on our meeting this morning three times, but I gather there is more to the story. Would you like to fill me in?"

Moncrief sipped her coffee and tore the horn off one end of her pastry. "We have an appointment with Lundqvist Investments, run by the Lundqvist family. My family has worked with theirs for decades; they're old money but relatively new on the magical scene—they can only trace their lineage back three generations on their mother's side. They bolstered their standing through influential marriages, and it didn't hurt that they came through the war relatively unscathed despite staying in Europe."

Neutrality pays off, he thought. It was the sort of thing Wilson would say to Moncrief, but Westwood would most certainly keep it to himself.

She started on her fruit cup and bit into an incredibly sweet piece of melon before continuing. "We are seeing Karl, the youngest of the three Lundqvist brothers. He is a self-made man via programming and software."

Wilson raised an eyebrow.

"Well, as much as anyone born to wealth can be self-made," Moncrief allowed. "He was brought back into Lundqvist Investments after his father passed; a bit of a scandal, considering everyone assumed Magnus would take it over after his death. Apparently, Magnus didn't approve of the situation, but it really was for the best. Magnus is a rock—solid, dependable—but he lacks a certain imagination."

She daubed a bit of strawberry jam in the flaky layers of her croissant, savored her last bite, and approved of the preserve. "Karl is charming, but confident to a fault, and neither he nor Magnus know that much about magic nor how to defend against it. The middle brother, Hans, seems to be the only one that really took to practicing the arts, but he's…" she searched for the right word, "quirky. Incredibly smart and a natural magician, but he has a hard time with social cues and behaving appropriately. They went through more than a handful of nannies during his formative years before he was sent to boarding school.

"That's where you come in." She motioned to him as she finished her coffee. "Your expertise in mundane and magical security is uniquely apt for what appears to be plaguing Lundqvist Investments."

"What makes you think they'll bring in an outside man?" Wilson asked.

"You work for me, an old family friend—hardly an outsider!" She feigned indignation. "Plus, Karl's got hooks," she pointed out with a sweet smile. "Despite the fraternal reunion after the death of the Lundqvist paterfamilias, he's still got a chip on his shoulder when it comes to his family; the best way to get in with Karl is for Magnus to disapprove. A little social and financial leverage on my part should be all it takes in the shadow of a Russian menace."

If dimples could kill, Wilson thought to himself as Moncrief beamed a self-satisfied smile. There were few better trained for social warfare than Clover. "And if that doesn't work?" he skated carefully on thin ice.

"Then we spend a few days in Monaco," she jauntily answered before lowering her voice. "Hobgoblin is on standby." Wilson nodded in comprehension: if Westwood couldn't get in via the business, he might get brought in as private security if the youngest Lundqvist lost one of his personal yachts due to an explosion. Hobgoblin wasn't subtle, but he was effective.

He sat back and integrated this new information with what was in the files. Once the Salt Mine analysts knew what to look for, they easily made the connection between the water elemental attacks, nearby proximity to one of Karl's yachts, and the network of sea cables laid out across the world's oceans. The trading algorithms pulled off the memory stick had an anticipated time delay built in, so it was pretty obvious how Lundqvist Investments managed to out-perform their peers: they cheated. *They'd just call it a competitive advantage, of course.*

Still, Wilson knew he was missing something. The remains of the attunement circle among the Nemo wreckage was not the work of a novice. Had Karl learned a few things from his older brother or had someone else crafted the circle? Wilson knew he was looking for a magical item, and a unique one if it required ritual attunement. It stood to reason that it traveled with Karl, based on the scattered geographical locations of the attacks, which meant Wilson had to get close enough to suss it out and retrieve it, preferably with the Ivory Tower taking the rap to cover his tracks.

With breakfast finished, everyone onboard strapped in for a smooth landing in fair weather. The Principality of Monaco was tiny, a sovereign city-state second only to the Vatican for smallest county in the world. Coming in at two square kilometers—less than one square mile—it didn't even have its own airport, which was why Moncrief's jet touched down at Nice Cote d'Azur Airport in Nice, France. After the heiress's staff unloaded her considerable luggage onto their transport, Wilson played his part and ushered Moncrief across the border.

With a reputation as the playground of the rich, Monaco wasn't really Wilson's scene but traveling in the style to which the Moncrief family was accustomed made it more palatable, even if his alias was hired help. The fifteen-mile drive into Monaco was breathtaking: picturesque boulevards with the coastline peeking out between buildings and foliage. There was no question why the Lundqvist brothers had relocated the company there; if a tax haven in a non-European Union country still solidly in Western Europe wasn't enough, the idyllic climate and weather was reason aplenty. As part of the French Riviera, Monaco occupied a prized piece of real estate sandwiched between France and the Mediterranean Sea, and spitting distance from the Italian border. It was where sunny and warm overlapped with European and a far cry from the cold snowy winters of Sweden.

After checking in at their hotel, they made their way to Lundqvist Investments's executive offices—the penthouse of a high-rise overlooking the sea. A stunning assistant escorted them into a sleek meeting room that overlooked the water and offered them beverages. Wilson scanned his environs while they waited for their cucumber-infused water; it was always the most expensive places that offered complimentary things and called it "service."

The decor could only be described as "seaside chic," which was the polite way of saying kitschy but expensive. The pair kept their cover in silence, uncertain if they were being watched or recorded. Moncrief took a seat at the table, and Wilson stationed himself behind her where he could see both the door and the windows. *Think, think, think...* Wilson summoned his will and sent out feelers to perceive what could not be seen.

Within ten minutes, Karl Lundqvist entered the room with a burst of energy. At six feet tall, he towered over Moncrief and Wilson, and his carefree demeanor matched his sun-bleached blond hair and tanned skin. Barrel-chested and good-looking, he was hardly the image one expected of a programmer; he reminded Wilson of a walking life-sized Ken doll. "Alicia! How good to see you again." He was all smiles and cheer but his blue eyes cut briefly to Wilson, assessing the unknown man in the room.

"Likewise, Karl," she acknowledged him, and they exchanged two kisses on alternating cheeks. Moncrief paid no mind to Wilson; as her hired man, he was an accessory, just like her handbag or her sunglasses.

Lundqvist followed her cue, "Please, take a seat." The two blondes sat opposite each other while Wilson stood and continued his vigilance. "What brings you into town?"

"Officially? The beaches and casinos," Moncrief replied once she had settled back into her chair.

"And unofficially?" Lundqvist inquired with a roguish grin as he poured himself some water from the carafe.

"There's talk that you've pissed off the wrong people, Karl," she chided him, "and I'm here to make sure it isn't true."

"Believe nothing of what you hear and only half of what you see," he aphorized before doubling down on his breezy facade. "So what have the wagging tongues been saying?"

"That you have a Russian problem," she tactfully eluded to recent events.

"Alicia, I didn't know you cared," he teased and put his hand over his heart.

"My concern lies chiefly with my family's holdings. I need to know they are secure," she swatted off his puerile attempt to bait her. "Not that I'm not terribly fond of you," she added sweetly.

Lundqvist straightened up and became more serious—the Moncriefs were a weather vane among the upper echelon of old magical money. If they pulled out of the company, it wouldn't be long before other families and organizations followed suit. "I assure you, Alicia, we have things well in hand."

Unmoved, Moncrief choose her next works carefully.

"While your more conventional clientele may be satisfied with your measures, investors with more esoteric assets are less reassured. When one tangos with Russia, one dances with the Ivory Tower. Would you even know if you were subject to magical attack?"

Lundqvist's eyes flickered to Wilson once more at her open mention of such things, and Moncrief took that as her cue. "This is Westwood. He does private security for me, and I would consider his endorsement of the situation most comforting." She waved her hand to Wilson, who procured something from an inner pocket. He placed a card with just a phone number on it in front of Lundqvist.

The Swede noted Wilson's gloved hand and the hint of a concealed weapon. "Alicia, I'm not sure if Magnus will agree to—"

"I'll be in Monaco for five days. That should give your people plenty of time to make the appropriate arrangements." Her voice retained her gaiety and lightness, but there was a note of finality in her tone. This was not a suggestion or negotiation. It was an order.

Moncrief rose and Lundqvist reflexively stood as well and accepted her outstretched hand. "So good to see you again, Karl. Give my best to your family." Wilson opened the door and Moncrief sashayed out.

Chapter Fourteen

"You smell worse than a Killakee cat," Grizel Greedigut hollered as Lukin passed through his door. The aroma was so rank, the imp lost his appetite and dropped his pirozhki.

"Surströmming accident," Lukin lied. "What's your excuse, Griz?" the agent fired back. Normally he would have cleaned up before reporting, but the retrieval of Zarubin's bag from the *Yantar*'s wreckage was too important for him to take the time to clear up the olfactory landmine he'd stumbled upon. Lukin had found a trace of residual magic he couldn't identify, but imps had abilities that Lukin didn't.

"You smell like you fornicated with three-day-old sushi," Greedigut slung another insult with glee.

"If you must know, I had to catch a ride back on a fishing vessel or wait another three days for the next lift off the salvage ship," he again lied as an explanation. The imp was remarkably ignorant of modern transportation methods and wouldn't question the response. Normally Lukin didn't lie directly to the imps, but if the imp network ever found out about his misstep, he'd never hear the end of it. While fellow agents of the Ivory Tower understood the occasional miscalculation, the little devils were not so forgiving or sympathetic.

"I believe the Interior Council would want to know more about this." He hoisted an orange bag onto the table. It smelled significantly better than its bearer despite its own odor of fishy, salty damp. "I need you to ask around and see what you can find out about the residual magic in there."

Greedigut wiped his hands on a dirty handkerchief and smacked his lips. "Can I keep anything non-magical?" He had a penchant for trinkets and souvenirs.

Lukin shrugged. "As long as it's not important to the mission, I don't see why not." He had already cleared out the valuables for himself.

The imp tucked the crumpled square of fabric into his pocket and climbed up on the table to get a closer look at the bag. "Go take a shower and get a shave," he suggested before jamming his head into the bag. "I've got this."

Lukin didn't respond as he felt somewhat shamed—he was getting grooming tips from a bearded, pot-bellied fiend! "You'll call me the second you know something?" he asked point blank. Even though liberated imps were under contract, Lukin preferred an explicitly stated arrangement of service; they were still devils and bound to their word.

Greedigut dismissively waved his hand. "Of course. Now stop stinking up my workshop." Lukin slunk out of the basement; he had an appointment with some dried skunk glands, a long hot shower, and an ice-cold vodka.

Once he was alone, the imp spent a moment playing with the zippers on the bag, relishing the sound of them going up and coming undone. He eventually pulled himself away from his entertainment and rummaged through what remained of Andrei Vasilovich Zarubin's possessions. He tossed the clothing aside, but not before checking the pockets and patting down every square inch; some of his favorite finds had been things unearthed with a seam ripper. The prolonged submersion had ruined the toiletries, but the travel shaving kit was in good repair, not that he would ever consider shaving his signature beard.

Next, the imp thumbed through the wrinkled and warped pages of a collection of Rilke's poems; Greedigut didn't have this one, so he placed it aside for inclusion on his bookshelf as a little minor magic could make the book usable again. Finally, he reached the last of it: a tin box shaped like a miniature steamer trunk covered in vintage stamps. Like a child on Christmas Eve, he held the package to his ear and shook it; the jangle of possibility sparked joyful anticipation. His short stubby fingers carefully pried off the top, revealing a hodgepodge of small items.

The deck of cards was ruined despite the wax coating, but a pair of dice looked fine, and after a few test rolls, the imp decided they were loaded and still rolling crooked. *These could come in handy*, he thought as he pocketed the dice. There was a nub of an eraser, a three-inch stub of pencil whose end had been chewed to bits, a multi-tool, and a few small bits of clockwork that didn't seem to belong to anything.

As the imp pulled the items out of the box, a small jolt seared his fingertips when he touched one of the small pieces of clockwork—a spark of magic that completed its arc at his touch. He pulled out a loupe and examined the mechanism, turning one gear and then another to see how it operated as a single piece. Everything moved lockstep as the rotating teeth drove each other to no discernable effect.

He squatted on the edge of the table, opened up the desk drawer, and pulled out a bottle of vodka. Given his size, he struggled with it, but the cap eventually came off. He filled a small glass to the brim and cleansed his palate with the oversized shot of vodka before licking the piece of clockwork. A cold metallic tang permeated his palate with a twist of burnt citrus at the end. It was like tasting the color purple.

"Shit," Greedigut cursed aloud. Not only was it something unfamiliar to him, but he was going to have to go deep to get answers. He poured himself another drink and ran through his mental Rolodex. The secret to Greedigut's long career as a liberated imp was mindful cultivation of his contacts: ask the right imp the right question, always bring a gift, and don't tap the same vein twice in a row. Over the years, he had assembled an encyclopedic array of which relations—well, of those still speaking to him, of course—were the best for a particular information request, and what their favored mortal delicacy was.

Greedigut plucked out a name and tidied himself for his incipient visitor by straightening his hair and picking out the bits of food and debris that had fallen into his beard. He searched his numerous shelves and caches before finding the appropriate offering. Next, he locked the door to the room before entering his small summoning circle. While most summoning circles were designed to protect the caster from the creature it called forth, the Ivory Tower modified them for liberated imps so that they had to be inside the circle to summon another imp for information. It was a clever safeguard to prevent them from summoning anything too nasty into the mortal realm, because the imps couldn't leave the circle if there was anything else in it with them.

Humans were often trickier than devils, the small fiend thought to himself before he chanted his spell, naming his kin. Unlike mortal summoners, he needed no blood offering as he was calling one of his own. Within a matter of minutes, a crouched figure appeared in the circle with him and rebuked him by name. "Grizel Greedigut! You'll be the death of me, summoning me here without warning."

Spixi the Crooked had been old as long as he could remember, but that had never stopped her from tanning his hide. Technically, she was shorter than him by a few inches but when she spoke, she might have been two feet tall for the effect it had on Greedigut. His knees knocked behind his beard, and the hairs on the back of his neck stood erect.

"Aunty! It's so good to see you. It's been too long," he crooned unctuously.

The elder imp swept away a greasy lock of hair and turned her good eye on him. "What do you want?"

"Do I need a reason to visit with my favorite aunty?" he asked rhetorically with friendliness in his tone, but he was wise enough to keep his distance.

His charm was met with a tight-lipped smirk. "You silver-tongued devil, you think you can fool me?! I pulled you out of the birthing pit myself; one look at your face, and I can tell if you pissed or shat."

Greedigut performed the next stage of their kabuki and admitted defeat. "You may be old, Aunty, but I see you're still sharp as a tack. In all honesty, I ran into something strange in the mortal realm and I need your expertise to understand what is going on. I don't think anyone else can help me, so my apologies for disturbing you."

She beamed triumphantly; flattery always worked with Spixi. "Now the truth comes out! And what's in it for me?"

He tossed a dark tan box labeled "Terva Leijona" in her direction, and she caught it in motion and sliced it opened with her razor-sharp nails, curled under like a talon from the contracture of her ancient hands. A cluster of small, round, black biconcave discs spilled into her other hand. "You remembered!" she cackled with equal parts shock and delight.

"How could I forget?!" he simulated affection.

Spixi carefully poured them back into the box and popped one into her mouth. It watered on contact with the smoky pine tar mixed with the salty, astringent salmiak. The box disappeared on her person and she spoke resolutely, "All right, let me take a look at what you have."

Greedigut presented the clockwork to her and placed it in her hands. Her eyes might not be so good anymore, but her other senses were still in fine working form. She caressed the machinery, smelled it, tasted it. When her physical senses could glean no more, she cupped the intricate interlocking pieces of metal in her wizened hands and murmured a few words. Her demeanor suddenly shifted, and even though it turned friendly, it made him nervous. "Why my Grizel, you have been up to no good! I *knew* the claims that you had gone soft were rubbish."

The knot in Greedigut's stomach grew larger and squeezed tighter the more her pride shone through her face. "What is it, Aunty?"

Her wide-mouthed grin prominently displayed her remaining teeth. "Time magic, my boy. It's time magic."

Chapter Fifteen

It had been a little over a week since the *Yantar* sank and only five days since his return to Corktown, but Alex Husnik was already bored and restless. After a weekend getting to know Martinez over good food and bad TV, he almost felt normal again, but then Monday morning came. There wasn't anything wrong with the set-up: he had the house to himself during the day, the food was good, the pain was manageable, and as far as housemates went, Martinez was amenable company. No doubt, the situation was ideal for convalescence. The problem was that Husnik was terrible at doing nothing by himself and he had another seven weeks of this. He had no idea how Wilson did it for months after the attack at Utashinai. *Of course, he hadn't been completely alone*, Husnik reminded himself. *He had me.*

Dying was always an option for a Salt Mine agent, and in some situations, it wasn't necessarily the worst choice. Husnik had long since chalked it up as an occupational hazard for himself, but when he'd seen the specter of death lingering over Wilson, it wasn't an option any longer. Despite how things shook out, he'd never doubted saving him was the right thing to do, even if it'd complicated things.

Husnik had promised himself that when his number was called, he wouldn't be one of those that hung around after the fact. He had nothing against Millie and Wolfhard, but they only confirmed what he had always felt: the one good thing about dying was the complete surrender of one's grasp on the living world and all its baggage. Why bother with how you died, who showed up at your funeral, or what happened to your stuff? You're dead—let it go. Husnik's problem was that even though he had died twice—once allegedly as himself and once again as Boris Mikhailovich Petrov—he was still alive and he'd left behind a mess on both counts.

Husnik had done what was expected of him. Deep cover was part of his job and when the opportunity to infiltrate the premier Russian spy ship arose, he was the natural choice. His Russian was flawless, he had naval experience, and he was the best social chameleon of the bunch. He was pretty sure saying no to Leader wasn't an option; what he hadn't cared to admit to anyone—especially himself—was that he'd never considered turning it down at the time. She had given him an easy way out of an untenable situation.

Things were never the same between him and Wilson after the run-in with the karakuras, and taking the assignment seemed easier than slugging it out. It had been a chance to start over as someone else. Part spy, part method actor, Husnik breathed life into his aliases and embodied who they were. One of his favorite parts of deep cover was absorbing his backstory and magically adjusting his tattoos to fit the bill, not just for utility but to support the narrative. For those five years, he didn't have to carry the weight of Alex Husnik's sins and inadequacies, but he should have known better. Karma's a bitch and magic wasn't the only reason it would get you.

He readjusted himself on the sofa and lowered the volume of the TV. He knew Wilson knew he was alive, and everyone was conspicuously not talking about it. The fact that Wilson was out on a mission was just the cherry on top of the ironic sundae. In retrospect, he understood that while he hadn't done anything wrong, it certainly wasn't fair or kind. He'd had time to prepare for his departure. He knew it was the last fight, the last make-up, the last kiss, the last embrace, the last night on the couch watching TV in each other's arms. Time and space from the situation had given him clarity: he'd made Wilson mourn him alone. "At very least, I owe him an apology," he said to the vapid program playing in the otherwise empty house, "if he'll even speak to me."

Before he could become any more maudlin, Husnik switched off the television and turned on music. *I've been Russian for too long*, he chided himself as he took to his crutches and swung his way into the kitchen. He opened the fridge and pantry and assessed supplies. He didn't want to use anything Martinez might need for whatever she had planned, but he wanted to do something nice for someone.

"Brownies," he eventually uttered. "I have everything I need for brownies. Who doesn't love brownies? Even Satanists love brownies." The empty room didn't argue and he started laying everything out on the counter, reciting the recipe he'd made a hundred times. He leaned back on a high chair, using his good leg to stabilize his descent, and started sifting the lumps out of the cocoa powder. The brown flecks dusted the pristine mixing bowl and soothed his bruised conscious. *Maybe I'm getting wiser with age*, he pondered before dismissing the notion with a good laugh at himself as he reached for the flour. *And maybe water's getting less wet...*

Chapter Sixteen

The three Lundqvist brothers rode in silence as their sleek limousine crossed into Nice. Like their ride, they were dressed in formal black to attend a charity event. Magnus didn't understand why they couldn't have just sent a check and stayed home, while Hans questioned why he had to wear a tux to save the ocean—it certainly didn't care about his attire. Karl, however, understood the significance; they were there to see and be seen. He didn't admit as much to his brothers, but Moncrief's talk of unrest among the wealthy magical elite had jarred him, enough to have his personal assistant call the number on the card and arrange for Westwood to tour the company's facilities bright and early Monday morning. In times like this, it was important to show a united front publicly— show that everything was business and pleasure as usual, and there was no need to panic because all was normal—which was why he'd extended an invitation to Alicia Moncrief to tonight's fundraiser.

Wrangling his family to fall into line required more than a phone call from his assistant. A suggestive word to Magnus's wife was generally all it took to get him into his monkey suit, but the publicity from the recent hack and subsequent uptick in client-relation maintenance had made him prickly; his reservoir of patience and charm was quickly being outstripped by demand. Luckily, Camille never needed much of a reason to put on a pretty dress and drink a little too much champagne, and she had a way of smoothing over Magnus's ruffled feathers—no one knows what a marriage is really like except for the people in it.

The only reason Hans had agreed to come was because the event was being held at the aquarium. Hans held a deep affection for creatures of the sea and it was a subject he and Karl bonded over. What others found cold and alien, Hans regarded with warm curiosity and respect. Since it was an exclusive closed-door event, and the exorbitant price of admission limited the number of people in the typically packed venue, Hans was looking forward to the better communion with the aquatic residents. This suited Magnus, as Hans was relentless with gaffes and faux pas, and the more time he spent with the fish and resident octopus, the better.

"You look lovely tonight, Camille," Karl complimented his sister-in-law's stunning gown.

"Thank you, Karl," she replied gracefully. "It's nice *someone* noticed." The insinuation rolled over Magnus, who had long since stopped listening to his wife.

"It makes you look like a betta fish," Hans commented

earnestly on the pattern of the sequins on the bodice and the colorful flounce and train that draped when she stood.

Camille smiled knowingly. "That's sweet, dear, but you can simply tell a lady that she looks nice. You don't have to be so specific." Hans nodded. He didn't mean to be difficult, he simply had a hard time following other people's rules when they were illogical or irrational, and sadly, social convention was often both.

"You're wasting your breath, Camille," Magnus sneered. "The less time we spend there, the less chance Hans can screw up. Two drinks, one check, and we're out." Hans began nervously pulling at his cuff links under the comment: they suddenly didn't seem to want to work properly.

"Does that include the scotch in your hand, Magnus?" Karl retorted. "You're more than welcome to leave after you make an appearance, but I intend to enjoy the evening fully and welcome anyone else who joins me."

"Here, let me," Camille offered gently and lay her hands on Hans's forearm. He calmed down a measure and she straightened his cuffs.

Magnus teetered on the edge and choose unkindness. "Figures you two would stick up for the imbecile."

"Don't call him that," Karl said flatly, dropping all his charm. "He contributes to this family as much as anyone," he alluded to Hans's esoteric work. Without him, Karl would have never figured out which of his trophies were magical or how to use them. Hans wasn't stupid; he just thought differently, and neither his father nor Magnus knew what to do with him. They provided for him and left him alone with his interests to become the largely forgotten Lundqvist brother, until Karl reentered the picture to become his brother's keeper after their father's death.

Camille and Hans kept physical contact, grounding each other from the growing tension in the cab. Magnus scoffed, "You sound just like Mother." Content to get the last word in, he quieted down for the rest of the car ride, much to everyone's relief. Camille and Karl lightened the mood and Hans slowly let his older brother's animosity seep out of him.

Hans had always been their mother's favorite, as the only one of her sons with both the skill and proclivity for magic. It didn't spare him from nannies and boarding school, but it bought him a lot of leeway from his father's wrath and expectations. "At least he knows how to practice the arts," had become the rallying cry of his defense, even long after their mother had passed.

Karl had a soft spot for his idiosyncratic brother, attributing the beginning of his affinity for the water to the countless hours Hans had spent telling him about the sea during their childhood. While Magnus was off being groomed to play "little master," they were often left to amuse themselves under the semi-watchful eye of governesses until they were old enough to be sent to school. As they got older and their ill-fit into the family became more apparent, it had become their lingua franca, an overlapping of interest that salvaged many a family event for the two of them.

While the Nemo Sea Lab was funded and executed by Karl, it had been in part inspired by conversations he'd had with Hans over the years. Hans had a fascination with the idea of living under water and the research lab was one step closer to that becoming a reality. Even after Hans had set up the attunement circle for Karl, he took every opportunity to accompany his brother to the lab. Hans had taken the Nemo's destruction badly in a guttural way, like the world had been lessened with it gone. Besides the optics of tonight, Karl had hopes that the aquarium would help give his brother's troubled soul a little solace.

The car pulled up to the entrance and the inhabitants readied themselves for presentation. Just as they straightened collars and seams, they ironed out all traces of internecine strife with bright eyes and smiles. Even Hans managed to produce a near facsimile of the face people make when they are happy. He had practiced for years to get the "happy face" right.

The aquarium was modest in size, but what it lacked in space it compensated for in ambiance. The family-oriented tourist destination transformed into a cozy chic space after hours with minimal sleight of hand. With the gift shop and ticket counters closed and the overhead lights lowered, the lobby was a place to greet and mingle before venturing deeper into the winding interconnected rooms. The creatures of the deep crept out of their cracks and crevasses and the undulations of the jellyfish danced under diffuse spotlights. The tunnel of fish gleamed brighter in contrast, and the oohs and aahs heightened whenever a shark or ray skated by. The floating trays of cocktails and hors d'oeuvres kept the formally attired guests in good spirit as the bright whites of their shirts glowed while they milled through black-lit rooms.

Hiding in plain sight behind flutes of champagne was Nalin Buchholz—Salt Mine codename Hobgoblin. When Hobgoblin heard he'd be backing up Wilson and Moncrief on the Côte d'Azur, he imagined *he* would be the one gallivanting in the tuxedo. Wilson generally preferred to stay in the background, and no one had ever accused Hobgoblin of being a wallflower. However, Wilson had already established himself as the infiltrator, which was how Hobgoblin found himself in disguise as part of the wait staff. Hobgoblin wasn't sure which bothered him more: the fact he was playing a waiter while Wilson accompanied Moncrief to a black tie event, or that he had to wear an unflattering wig and prosthetic nose as part of his disguise. His only consolation was that everyone agreed that, left to his own devices, he was too pretty to be serving drinks and had to dial down his roguish good looks with a disguise. Being tall, dark, and handsome was his cross to bear and he made it look good.

Camille's shimmering blue dress caught Hobgoblin's eye

first. She was escorted on the arm of her husband with her brothers-in-law in tow. Hobgoblin dropped off his empty tray and murmured an exaggerated "they're here" under his breath.

"You better be talking about the Lundqvist clan because I'm not dressed to fend off a poltergeist," Moncrief's hushed voice quipped in through his earpiece.

"I am," Wilson curtly replied. "Now cut the nonessential chatter."

Hobgoblin straightened the starched white linen over his forearm and balanced the full tray on his hand. He mentally mapped his trajectory to the newcomers, but before he could make contact, a very excitable Frenchwoman preempted his approach. "Camille, I'm so glad you could come. Your gown is absolute striking." They exchanged a shallow embrace and air kisses as to preserve their hair and makeup.

Hans took a step back, feeling somewhat accosted by the vitality and ardor of her unbridled greeting, and left to find the cephalopods. Magnus excused himself as quickly as he could after delivering his wife to the party's hostess—he waited just long enough to see she had a glass of champagne in her hand before making a beeline toward the bar.

Karl stepped up to occupy the space evacuated by both his brothers. "Yvonne, the place looks marvelous. You've outdone yourself," Karl praised the event organizer. "I would have never guessed a gaggle of sticky-fingered children was roaming the building a few hours ago."

"Nothing a little elbow grease and disinfectant can't fix." She offered him her hand for a demure kiss.

More like she stood around and ordered everyone else to clean, Hobgoblin commented to himself while he kept his mien neutral. He circulated the entryway, keeping tabs on the respective Lundqvists. "Magnus at the bar, Hans at the octopus, Karl and his brother's hot wife entering the fish tunnel," he whispered once he found a private niche.

"I've got Magnus," Moncrief called dibs as she did a quick primp using the wall of glass between her and the fish of the Amazon.

"Heading to the octopus," Wilson muttered as he abandoned his perch in the shadowy corner designed for the bevy of giant deep-water crabs.

"I'll keep Karl warm for you," Hobgoblin swapped out trays—this one bearing an assembly of prawn and avocado amuse-bouche—and entered the Plexiglas tunnel.

*****

The cash bar was just past the lobby—close enough for a hasty break upon entry and convenient for fast retrieval once the rest of one's party was ready to depart. Populated almost exclusively by bored spouses and companions, the mood was indifferent with a hint of discontent. In bygone years, the collective smoke from their cigarettes and cigars would have shrouded them in a flimsy veil separating them from the festivities.

The other agents always gave Clover a hard time about her prodigious amount of luggage—when was she going to spontaneously need a formal gown with matching accessories? *Tonight*, she thought smugly, answering their remembered ribbings as she walked up to the bar. As she aimed her gait toward one side of Magnus, the simple lines of her diaphanous dress shifted with the swing of her hips and the beaded detail on the bodice shimmied with each sway of her bare shoulders.

Everyone was acutely aware of her, but the bartender was the only person who could openly acknowledge her approach—it was boorish to leer at an heiress in polite company. She ordered a drink that would project her affected mood, "Rusty nail, neat." Happy, content people didn't wind up at the bar at these sort of events.

Magnus had long mastered the art of looking at women without being obvious and snuck a glance at the glimmer in his periphery. *A serious drink for such a frivolous girl*, Magnus mentally noted as he waited for an appropriate moment to make himself known. "Hello Alicia."

He had the air of someone seeking respite, so she spared him the socialite pantomime: cheek kisses, exaggerated excitement, and mindless small talk. They were just two acquaintances who found themselves at the same bar. She looked up and feigned surprise, "Ah, Magnus, I didn't see you there. I wouldn't have guessed this was your sort of thing." She matched the tenor of his demeanor.

"You'd have guessed right. This is more my brother's style, but Camille seemed excited at a night out."

The bartender delivered her cocktail and she proposed a toast, "The things we do for family." He met her sparkling blue eyes and raised his glass to hers.

"What brings you here?" he made conversation as the man behind the counter brought him another.

"At the fundraiser or the bar?" she asked enigmatically.

Magnus shrugged his broad shoulders. "Either. Both."

"Your brother invited me, and it would have been rude not to accept. Being a Moncrief has its responsibilities and an open checkbook for charitable causes is one of them," she quipped. "To be perfectly honest, I'm not even sure what this event is for. Saving the beaches? The coral reefs? The whales?"

Magnus laughed, and his posture relaxed. He opened his torso and tilted toward her. "I haven't the foggiest, but they have scotch, so it's not all bad."

"And Drambuie," she said, gently tilting her drink to her perfect lips and pausing just long enough to add, "I'll drink to that."

*****

"Look at all those tentacles," one woman commented

insipidly to her friend over champagne.

"Are octopuses the ones with eight or ten legs?" her friend asked as she tried to take a better picture of the cephalopod with her phone.

"Eight," the original woman spoke authoritatively. "Squid are the ones with ten legs and squirt ink."

"I thought octopuses had ink, too," her friend replied without neglecting her mobile.

"I don't think so…" The first woman now sounded dubious.

"I'm pretty sure I've eaten octopus ink at a restaurant," she pressed.

"They use squid ink in food, maybe that's what you're thinking of?" They juggled their drinks and consulted their phones.

Wilson silently watched from behind: the chatty patrons furiously tapping thumbs to screens, the giant Pacific octopus indifferent to their ignorance, and Hans Lundqvist sending them eye daggers from the side but saying nothing.

"No, you're right. Octopuses have ink," the original speaker conceded defeat and tucked her phone back into her clutch. "I wonder what it's thinking?" she spoke in a dreamy tone. Wilson could almost see the proverbial smoke steaming out of Hans's ears.

"She," Wilson curtly spoke.

The two ladies turned their heads, as did Hans. "Excuse me?"

"That's a female giant Pacific octopus," he informed them as he stepped forward.

The ladies exchanged looks, nonverbally coming to a consensus on how they felt about the interloper. "How can you tell?" one of them skeptically inquired.

"Well, first, the octopus is named Calliope. Second, she doesn't have a hectocotylus," Wilson argued and veered to the side of the pair not occupied by Hans.

"A what?" the other queried.

"An octopus penis," Wilson opted for vernacular language, and he caught the start of a smile on Hans's face in his periphery. "And third, that"—he pointed to thin curtain of white beads streaming in the current—"is a strand of eggs."

"She's going to be a mum!" the older one squealed.

"Unlikely," Hans finally spoke, startling the pair of women. "They are probably not fertilized. This octopus has been here for almost two years, and the only way the eggs could be inseminated would be in the wild."

"So she's taking care of these eggs for nothing?" the younger one pouted.

Wilson selected his words for maximum effect. "She's taking care of the eggs because that's what she's programmed to do." Based on the abrupt change in body language, he'd chosen wisely. "Don't worry, she'll be dead soon. Octopuses don't live long after reproducing, even if the eggs are duds."

Sandwiched between the two odd men, something finally

pinged on the ladies' radar; the urge to be somewhere better lit with more people nearby took hold of them. "Let's go to the tunnel and see the fish of the Caribbean," one suggested to the other, who glommed onto the suggestion immediately.

As the women scurried out of the room, Wilson took a seat on the other end of the bench, giving Hans ample space but making it unlikely that anyone would elect to sit between them. A blissful silence fell over the room; it was quiet enough to hear the gurgle of the tank's water system. Wilson knew better than to spoil the moment with introductions; there would be time for that later. Hans was content to watch Calliope tend to her eggs and Wilson was happy to gather his will and gently probe Hans magically. *Think, think, think.*

*****

Moncrief was halfway through her second rusty nail when she realized Magnus wanted to speak with her for more than just the obvious reasons.

"So who's this Daniel and why haven't I heard of him?"

"Daniel?" she responded, taking a sip to gather her thoughts.

"Daniel Westwood, the security specialist you recommended. Karl told me about him, said he'd booked a tour of our main office on Monday?" Moncrief heard concern in his voice, which was a departure from the anger or annoyance she expected. If he was against it, it wasn't apparent to her keen eye.

"Oh, Westwood! Sorry, I only think of him as Westwood, not as Daniel. He's not a friendly man, you understand."

He nodded, waiting for more.

"Our family has been using him for nearly two decades now. Does all of our special security, and nary a problem in that time. He also does the security for a few other old families as well. Invite only."

"We're an old family," Magnus objected.

"Of course you are! I'm just saying he does the really old families, you know." Moncrief put on her sympathetic, but slightly patronizing, smile. "Point is, he's impeccable."

When Magnus accepted her assurance without flinching at her barb, she felt a knot in her stomach which had nothing to do with her alcohol consumption. Magnus was deeply concerned, so much so that he and Karl were working together amicably. *Perhaps things are worse than we know.*

Chapter Seventeen

Èze, France
25th of August, 02:29 a.m. (GMT+2)

"Hello?" Moncrief mumbled groggily before the phone even reached her cheek. She lay diagonally over the luscious sheets of the California king in her suite in the Château de La Chèvre d'Or. Outside the partially opened window, the sea rustled against the nearby rocky beach.

"Sorry to bother you, Alicia, but we have an emergency," Magnus said on the other side of the line.

"Emergency?" she asked, coming to clear consciousness in a second. *Did Hobgoblin jump the timeline on the emergency?*

"There was a break in. We tried calling Westwood, but the number didn't work. We thought you might know how to reach him."

We. She picked up his word choice. *So, Karl's involved as well.* "He does that. He burns any numbers he provides to prospective clients after he's arranged a date to meet. He's a bit odd that way, but I don't question his methods."

His grunt confirmed what Wilson had once told her: people love the appearance of security and are apt to confuse it with actual security. "Well, we'd like him to come over early, and you're welcome, too, of course," he added as an afterthought.

"How bad is it?" she inquired.

"I'd rather not say over the phone," he replied cryptically, "but we thought it couldn't wait until Monday. It would be preferable if he came immediately."

"Of course," she reassured him. "I know where he's staying. I'll get a hold of him. Be there in an hour?"

"I appreciate it, Alicia. We'll be at the tower waiting."

Moncrief threw on a robe and rang Hobgoblin down the hall to see if Leader had pushed up their timeline; she hadn't. Next, Moncrief called Wilson in the next room and explained the situation. Within fifteen minutes, Hobgoblin was steering the Firenze Red Range Rover through the quiet streets along the rocky coast toward Monaco.

Lundqvist Investments owned a twenty-two story building on the Boulevard d'Italie not far from the French Embassy in Monaco. The Lundqvist Building—as it had been rechristened—contained a dozen different businesses, but Lundqvist Investments occupied three-fourths of the floors. The top three-fourths of the floors, naturally.

Wilson had Hobgoblin circle the building a couple of times as he checked on the integrity of the exterior and Moncrief inspected the surrounding grounds. It wasn't the sort of place for a smash and grab, and only an idiot would hang around after a break-in, but he didn't want to rule anything out. Nothing seemed amiss to either of them, and after the third pass, they pulled into the underground parking facility. They were greeted by a parking attendant armed with a CZ 75.

After confirming their identity, he told them where to park and where the elevators were.

"He wasn't that well-armed three days ago," Moncrief mused.

Hobgoblin scoffed. "There wasn't even a guard at the booth when I scouted it out."

"When was that?" Wilson asked.

"Six days ago, before we leaked the fake hack."

"At least they're trying to become more conscientious about security," Wilson gave them credit in a moment of uncharacteristic generosity.

"Well, that was the plan, Mr. Security Specialist," Moncrief ribbed him.

"And you wonder why I'm not nicer…" Wilson muttered.

Hobgoblin smirked as he selected a parking spot. He had the pick of the lot at this time of night. He whipped the wheel and backed in like a pro—in their line of work, you never knew when you're going to need to make a quick exit. "Give me a ring if you need anything," he said, pulling out his phone and settling in while Moncrief and Wilson left the vehicle.

Moncrief could almost see the wave of unfriendliness that washed away all traces of Wilson as he adapted his Westwood role. Not that he was all that affable to begin with, but the verbal sparring partner she had moments ago was gone. They didn't speak on the ride up, and by the time the bell chimed for their destination, the transformation was complete.

As the elevator doors opened, both Karl and Magnus jutted

through for handshakes. "Thanks for coming, Alicia. Mr. Westwood," they said in near unison.

"What happened?" Moncrief asked.

"We had an unwanted visitor," Magnus took charge, leading them into the sleek meeting room they'd previously used. This time, a laptop occupied the end of the table. A single orange cable led into a wall outlet. Karl punched in a password to unlock the computer and waved his hand, indicating they should take a seat where they could see the screen.

"We detected the infiltrator at 1:44 this morning," Karl opened. "Lundqvist Investments's main office occupies fifteen floors of this building. We start on the fifth floor with a guest reception area, along with a café and eatery, a small gym, and a relaxation suite. From there, we have ten floors of traders that work the various world markets, equities, commodities, currencies, and so forth. The next four floors are all computer-oriented—it's where we run all of our proprietary trading algorithms—and the top two floors are for upper management. The fifth—"

"How many employees?" Wilson interrupted, even though he knew the answer from his briefing. It was what Westwood would ask—*get to the point.*

Karl was taken back, he was not used to being interrupted. "I believe we've fifteen hundred or so in this building."

Wilson nodded and Karl continued, "The fifth floor and the top floor are the only floors accessible without a keycard. The IT rooms are only accessible to IT employees and management.

We do that so—"

"IT was the target. Yes?" Wilson again interrupted. *Just tell us about the break-in.* Moncrief kept her composure; after all, this was just Westwood being himself. She caught Wilson in her periphery. His methods weren't her methods, but she couldn't fault him. He was fully inhabiting his role.

Between the hour of the night and the stress of the break-in, the interruptions to his carefully planned presentation had completely flustered Karl. Magnus made no attempt to hide his smirk. "I think Mr. Westwood would like to focus on the actual break-in and not the security plan of the building. That *is* why we called him out in the middle of the night," Magnus steered his youngest brother. "Karl, if you would?"

Karl clicked on the security footage and entered another password that released the surveillance screens. There were four images of a male figure. Each was blurry, like it was slightly out of focus, except that everything else in the frame was crystal clear. And then there was the aura emanating from him, a veritable rainbow of colors.

Despite the odd visual, Wilson immediately identified the man. The man on the screen was none other than Alexander Petrovich Lukin, which meant that Lundqvist Investments most definitely had an Ivory Tower problem. He kept his impassive mien and waited for Moncrief to glom onto their intruder. After a few seconds, he saw a flicker of recognition in her blue eyes, but a subtle shake of Wilson's head was all she needed to keep her cover.

"What a strange picture!" she exclaimed in her carefree heiress voice. "Do either of you recognize him?" she asked the Lundqvist brothers. Karl and Magnus shook their heads.

"Why isn't it video? Are you running single-image cameras?" Wilson quickly asked, his incredulity bringing all eyes to him and away from Moncrief, as intended.

"This was caught by the cameras outside the only entrance to our mainframe rooms," Karl said. "They're video, of course, but they malfunctioned and this was all we could pull from them."

"All four malfunctioned at the same time, in the same way?" Wilson incredulously asked.

"All of the cameras did—site wide. These four were the only ones that caught anything and they're the ones that triggered the alarm systems."

"What's with the aura?" Moncrief asked.

"They're special cameras that Hans made," Magnus answered. "They're partly magical and they're supposed to reveal true forms. Hans put them up as a protection against shapeshifting infiltration. I don't know the details; you'd have to speak with him."

"Don't worry, we doubled-checked them to make sure he didn't mess them up before we installed them," Karl added.

This time, both Fulcrum and Moncrief worked to keep their poker faces up despite the weight of the reveal. Magical cameras were a big deal, and the fact that neither of the Lundqvists thought anything of them was significant, indicating that they really were magically ignorant. Mixing magic and technology was *extremely* hard to do. The Salt Mine, even with its extended resources, had found only one magical practitioner that could do such: Harold Weber. Leader had recruited him and he functioned as the armorer for the agency. Finding another person who could do the same was like finding a needle in a haystack that a unicorn was grazing on.

"Then I'll need to speak with Hans," Wilson said neutrally. "To fully analyze the image, I need to know what it's supposed to do and how it does it."

Magnus checked his Rolex. "Hans wakes up at 5:23, so we've got a little more than an hour before we can bring him in."

"Why the delay?" Wilson asked. He had noted the absence of the middle Lundqvist when they exited the elevators and took the chance to find out more.

"You don't wake him up early," Magnus said emphatically— he'd been there and done that. "He's unmanageable if you do. Worthless."

Karl added delicately, "Hans has adjustment issues; he likes his schedule and routine."

Wilson raised an eyebrow. "It that going to be a problem?"

"As long as you don't take anything he says personally and you allow him some time to process, he's usually fine," Karl reassured him. "How about we give you a tour of the facility so that when you speak with Hans, you have a common framework for the discussion?"

Moncrief piped in. "Is this something I need to be in on, or shall I return to the hotel?"

"I think we can take it from here, Ms. Moncrief," Wilson affirmed as he rose from his seat. Her primary objective had been done—he was now in with the Lundqvists. She didn't need to be involved in this part of the job. In fact, it would be easier for both of them to maintain cover if she wasn't. "This will give us an opportunity to get to know each other better. They can show me around the site until Hans is roused, and there is always the matter of discussing my fee."

"Play nice, boys," Moncrief chided them playfully as she made her exit. She was alone on the elevator ride down trying to make sense of what she had just seen. Lukin was bad news. It meant that Ivory Tower involvement wasn't just a fiction created by Salt Mine. It meant she had to be more vigilant than ever to maintain her larger cover—the naive heiress that was duped into letting a Salt Mine agent into her business. It also meant that she might have a Wilson problem—he had a well-known hatred of his Russian counterpart.

"How'd it go?" Hobgoblin asked when she entered the SUV.

"Fulcrum's in place," she sighed.

"Isn't that what we wanted?"

She dropped the other shoe, "Lukin was the intruder."

"Fuck."

*****

Lukin fumed as he kept his vigil on the Lundqvist Building from the balcony of the Ivory Tower safe house in Château Périgord II, taking care to obscure his binoculars amongst the ridiculous plant that dominated the small space. It was sheer dumb luck that the Tower had a condo right outside his targeted building, and he'd welcomed the serendipity as he so rarely caught a break. He should have known better. As he watched, he did what he always did when a job went pear-shaped—play it back to see what he should have seen the first time.

His mission had been simple: plant a small phone-sized device in the IT room so the Ivory Tower could ascertain if time magic was part of Lundqvist Investments's operations. He didn't know exactly how it worked and didn't really care. All he needed to know was how to properly attach it to the computers and how to hide it from the casual viewer.

Lukin had resented having to infiltrate so quickly. Normally, he would have spent a week to case the target and observe site behavior during the night. However, once Griz said time magic, Lukin's orders became ASAP.

It wasn't like they'd sent him in blind. Lukin had the construction schematics of the building—stolen from the architects who worked on the remodel. He had the location of the many cameras inside and brought his electronic scrambler to take care of them. He'd even brought replacement batteries because there were so many. If things had gone as planned, he should have been able to walk in, plant the device in one of the

IBM z13s, and then get out—twenty minutes from entrance to exit.

As for esoteric safeguards, he had done a dry scout—a walk around the building to check for wards and other magical security. Then, he visited one of the businesses on the lower floors, granting him access to the interior to do the same. The fact that he found no magical protections in place should have been a relief, but under the circumstances, it made him suspicious. What kind of fool dabbles in time magic without taking greater precautions?

He'd been as cautious as possible with the short time frame he had been given, going in during the wee hours of Sunday morning. None of the businesses would be open until Monday morning. Before entering the building, he'd burned the karma to kaleidoscope himself—a masterful spell that ensured that anyone who saw him would see a different version of him. Any two people would give conflicting descriptions, and if a single viewer saw him at two different times, they would see two different versions. It made a solid identification impossible. Between that and his electronic scrambler, he'd figured he was safe.

And then an alarm went off just as he was about to enter the IT room, even though he had found no magical wards on his approach and had blasted the cameras with his scrambler. He'd legged it once the alarm sounded, easily passing undetected by the *tupoy chelovek* of a guard. He thought he'd have less than five minutes to get away before the police arrived, ten tops. But they never came. The streets were silent.

That piqued his curiosity. Why have an alarm if no one came? Within fifteen minutes, a car registered to Karl Lundqvist pulled into the garage, and the upper floors of the building came to full-spectrum florescent life. An hour later, a red SUV circled the building, but he couldn't get a good look inside because of the heavy tinting on the windows.

A familiar dread sunk into Lukin—something important was happening and the fact that he didn't know what it was or who was involved bothered him. This prompted him to keep watch for far longer than he would have and his patience was eventually rewarded when he saw three figures walking around the building's exterior in the dead of night. He repressed a curse when he saw it was Fulcrum walking with Magnus and Karl Lundqvist. He lowered his binocular and sat back, a little breath taken out of him. *How on earth was the Salt Mine involved in all this?*

Chapter Eighteen

Every morning, Hans Lundqvist woke at 5:23 a.m. sharp, unless he wasn't feeling well. Then he allowed himself to stay in bed longer. He brushed his teeth, washed his face, combed his hair, and got dressed. In that order. If he wasn't leaving the house, which he didn't do very often, he always wore the same thing: a blue button-down shirt, gray slacks, gray-on-blue argyle socks with thin red diamonds for a splash of color, and brown leather shoes that he wiped down every night and polished every twenty days. If it was cold, he wore a jacket or a sweater, but he'd had little use for such things once he moved to Monaco with the rest of his family.

Promptly at six, he would come down for breakfast. Often he would eat alone, but other times Magnus or Karl would be there, depending on their schedules and travels. Camille was almost never there. She liked to sleep in—she insisted on getting her beauty sleep. Considering she was the prettiest woman he'd ever seen, second only to his mother, he didn't question her methods.

Hans's breakfast was simple but filling: two soft boiled eggs with two slices of toast cut into three strips each, a banana, and a cup of Earl Grey tea—no milk, one cube of sugar. It was something that could be reproduced pretty much anywhere, and Hans liked routine. If things were just so, he didn't need to spend any of his time and energy making decisions on trivial things, like what to wear or what he was going to eat.

When Hans rounded the corner to the dining room, his normal spread was awaiting him, as were both his brothers and a third man. By the look of their well-worn clothes and haggard faces, they had been up for some time.

Karl rose from his coffee and greeted him. "Good morning, Hans. Did you sleep well?"

"Good morning, Karl. Good morning, Magnus. I slept fine. What's going on?" Hans spoke bluntly but not rudely. He took his seat despite the unexpected turn of events; if he dallied, his eggs would get cold.

"We have a visitor. This is Daniel Westwood," Karl introduced him.

Wilson stood and extended his arm. "Hans, nice to formally meet you."

"The man from the aquarium," Hans responded and shook Wilson's hand in two crisp movements with a perfectly timed release. It was precise and mechanical, like a metronome. "You know about cephalopods," he declared.

Hans touched the shells of the egg cups—they were still warm. He tapped his small spoon on the first egg and sheared off its top, revealing runny yolk but solid whites—just how he liked it. He put two dashes of salt and one dash of pepper and tucked in.

Wilson watched Hans intently and darted his eyes to Karl and Magnus. Their faces told Wilson this was all part of Hans's routine. Wilson interpreted Hans's statement as a question and answered accordingly. "I've spent a lot of my life underwater. I love diving."

"Me too. Treasure hunting," Hans answered curtly.

"So I've read," Wilson responded truthfully. The Lundqvist name had come into his purview not only in his mission briefing, but also in his own private aquatic interests. Karl and Hans were renowned treasure hunters, mostly as venture capital, but they also got their hands dirty from time to time. "The HMS *Lady Nelson* find was spectacular."

"Everyone thought it would be in the Timor Sea since it disappeared on route from Melville Island in 1825, but it wasn't," Hans said matter-of-factly.

"Found north of Timor in the Banda Sea, if I recall," Wilson added before sipping his coffee.

Hans turned to Wilson. "That's right." He held eye contact a few seconds too long to be comfortable before returning to his breakfast. His second egg beckoned.

"I had no idea you dove, Mr. Westwood," Karl marveled.

"I'm good at my job but there's more to life than work," he answered in a very unWilson-like fashion, but it was totally

Westwood; there was a reason he catered to the old magical families who had retained their wealth.

"Indeed," Karl replied warmly.

Magnus cleared his throat—sometimes he thought he was the only adult among his siblings. "Hans, we had a break-in at the Lundqvist Building last night and Mr. Westwood is helping us beef up security," he brought to conversation back on topic.

Hans stopped eating and tilted his head to the side. "Someone broke through my cameras." There was no distress in his voice. Wilson noted very little inflection at all; it was just a statement.

"No. In fact, your equipment was the only thing that caught him and triggered the alarm," Karl qualified Magnus's account.

Hans resumed eating.

"That said, whoever broke in now knows more about our security, and they will adapt before they try again," Magnus spoke. Wilson could see Magnus was really trying to speak his brothers' shared language, but it was definitely Greek to him. "Which is why Mr. Westwood is here. He's a *special* security expert. For families like us."

Hans's brow furrowed—there were lots of ways the Lundqvists were special. He wished Magnus would be more specific.

"What Magnus means, is that Westwood knows how to protect against magic."

Hans's face lit up. "You know how to cast?" It was the first hint of emotion Wilson had seen from the middle Lundqvist all morning.

Wilson kept his persona intact. "Yes, Hans. I know how to cast."

Hans mind raced with excitement. He hadn't been in the company of another practitioner since his mother died. He generally didn't like company—it often involved wearing different clothes, and projecting the appropriate affectation at the correct time through a swath of banal conversation that didn't interest him in the slightest. Hans shut down momentarily to process this information. Magnus and Karl kept drinking their coffee and waited until Hans picked up his banana and opened it just slightly at the top—he had regained himself.

"We showed Mr. Westwood around the building and familiarized him with the security measures in place," Karl picked up the conversation again. "He would like to talk to you about your contribution."

Hans nodded his head in comprehension. Everyone has different gifts, but everyone contributes—that's what his mother had always told him.

Hans took his spoon and carved bites of banana out of the peel. Wilson had honestly never seen someone eat a banana in such a fashion, but resisted the urge to gawk. "I can show you my workshop. After breakfast," Hans answered. "Mother always said it's the most important meal of the day."

Karl and Magnus beamed; as a general rule, Hans didn't take well to strangers. "Quite right! We should have something more substantial than coffee," Karl started speaking, locking it down before Hans could change his mind. "Magnus and I have other things to attend to, which should give you plenty of time to get to know each other." His phrasing made it seem like Wilson and Hans were having a play date.

As if on cue, a servant appeared next to Karl. "Scrambled eggs and bacon with toast, please."

"Make that two," Magnus chimed in.

"Would you like something, Mr. Westwood?" Karl asked.

"I'll have whatever you're having," Wilson replied.

Hans eventually finished his banana and sat back with his tea. He couldn't remember the last time all three Lundqvist brothers had breakfasted together. It was a departure from his routine, but perhaps he would have another cup of tea.

Chapter Nineteen

Detroit, Michigan, USA
25th of August 10:29 a.m. (GMT-4)

Leader was sitting at her desk, mulling over Fulcrum's report. Ivory Tower's break-in played well with establishing him into the Lundqvist's confidence, but Lukin's presence was not reassuring. He was one of the Ivory Tower's most experienced agents, a prized chess piece that wasn't sent on frivolous missions. She knew what Fulcrum wanted to hear: full steam ahead, get the mission done, and just make sure Lukin's death looks like an accident. She wanted more information, but it wasn't critical enough to expend another question from Furfur. If only Stigma's cover hadn't died...

Hans Lundqvist was an intriguing and unexpected find. Then again, she had never expected to discover Harold Weber either, but these things had a way of working out. Karma worked both ways.

Leader turned to *The Temptation of Saint Anthony* by Jan Brueghel the Elder, the only piece of art she had in her austere office. She lost herself in the intense stokes of lapis blue of the food bearer's shirt. He was caught unaware of the hungry wolf behind him, nipping at his wares. The buzz of the intercom sounded, and she pressed the button on her desk. "Yes?"

"A call on the secure line from Major General Nikolay Yastrzhembsky," LaSalle's pleasant tenor spoke over the intercom. Leader's pregnant pause followed, and he waited in silence for instruction.

"Patch him in, David," she spoke. Within seconds, the phone on her desk beeped and she picked up. "Major General? You *have* moved up in the world."

She heard a husky laugh on the other end. "You flatter me, Leader, but don't pretend you didn't know about my promotion."

"I'm sure I don't know what you mean," she swatted away his bait. "But I know you didn't call to reminiscence about old times. How can I help you?"

His voice turned serious and officious. "We have a predicament; both of our agents tripping over each other's feet trying to take care of this problem."

"And what problem is that?" she asked innocently.

"Are you really going to make me say it aloud, Zaika?" he purred into the phone.

She smiled. "Humor me."

He sighed. "Time magic."

Leader's face drained of all mirth. "Confirmed?"

"By our imps." Her mind immediately reprocessed everything she thought she knew about this mission, and in her quiet, Yastrzhembsky knew all was not right. "You didn't know," he surmised.

Leader recovered. "We came to the same objective by a slightly different path."

"Now that you know the gravity of the situation, surely you see the foolishness of working against each other," he reasoned.

"And what do you suggest, Nikolay?" She left the field open.

"A collaboration under the pact," he offered.

Leader bit the side of her bottom lip. "Until the time magic has been neutralized?"

"Plus the standard twenty-four hours after," he stipulated.

Leader weighed it in her mind: could they be trusted and what were the consequences of failure either way? "Let me reach out to my operative. Do not have your agent make contact with the target or my operative until I have had a chance to make my orders clear."

"Understood. I will have my agent stand down," he agreed.

Leader did time zone math. "Give me six hours. Sometime after that, my operative will contact your agent. Is there anything else?"

"Nyet, but it's good to hear your voice after all this time."

"You're getting sentimental in your old age, Kolya," Leader replied before hanging up.

It had to be time magic, Leader thought as she poured herself a drink. She swore that humanity had a death wish for all the creative ways it figured out how to snuff itself out:

warfare, disease, famine, hedonistic consumption, religion, nationalism, nuclear weapons, biologic weapons…and that was just the non-arcane stuff.

She wished she could say that practitioners were better, but they were still human—they just had a whole other tool set to monkey around with. Long before she was Leader, the community of practitioners had loosely policed itself, composing a list of seven forbidden magics, things that could tear the fabric of reality apart. Time magic was one of them. It was like playing Russian roulette—if you kept pulling the trigger, you would eventually get the bullet.

Back in 1962, when the world was preparing for nuclear war and the mundane world was seven minutes to midnight, Ivory Tower and Salt Mine were battling their own apocalyptic nightmare: a magician mixing in time magic to go back in time to stop the World Wars from ever happening. Considering how much the world had suffered in the fifty years prior, no one could blame him for the sentiment, just the method.

Those that were there knew how close they had come to failure, largely because everyone was siloed to their own agency, looking to protect their country's interest in the backdrop of the cold war. It was then that a pact was made between Salt Mine and Ivory Tower—should either side have a magically verified incident of forbidden magic, they would cease counter-operations against each other and work together until the magic was neutralized. After resolution, every operative had twenty-four hours to evacuate the area before relations returned to baseline.

Since its founding, the Chisinau Pact has been invoked three times. Leader didn't think it was too much to ask of humanity to go more than fifteen years without trying to annihilate itself, but she wasn't entirely surprised by the news. It was about time.

She dug into the active case files until she located the report on the drive Stigma recovered from the *Yantar*, and cursed out loud. It was staring at her this whole time.

She buzzed the intercom and LaSalle knocked twice before entering. "David, confirm with the mathematicians about the time delay built into the Lundqvist algorithm. Ready a line to Fulcrum. And can you please bring me two aspirin."

"Of course," he responded. He knew there was no need to ask if she wanted water to wash them down.

Chapter Twenty

Saint Roman, Monaco
25th of August, 04:42 p.m. (GMT+2)

"This is foolishness!" Lukin yelled into his phone. "The man wants to kill me. He's wanted to kill me for years."

Major General Nikolay Yastrzhembsky, General Secretary of the Ivory Tower's Interior Council responded in a soothing voice. "Sasha, Sasha, why so melodramatic? This is good news! They already have their operative in place. Let him take all the risks. All you have to do is stand down for the next five hours and forty minutes and wait for contact." Lukin heard him lean back in the soft leather chair he so favored.

"Melodramatic? The man is crazy. Relentless," Lukin emphasized.

"He's also a good soldier. He does what he's ordered, and he's been ordered to work with you."

"And you think I trust Leader more than Fulcrum?" Lukin scoffed. "You think there are not orders within orders?"

"On this matter we can trust her. She would not break the Chisinau Pact for your sorry hide," Yastrzhembsky insisted. "You've been around long enough to know the game."

"If you make me work with him, it's going to cost you,"

Lukin growled. "I'm not going to let my guard down for a single second, not a second. You're also going to have to expedite me some particular items I'll need. And you'll have to pay for those, too. Daily—not after I've returned and filed my paperwork. I'm not risking the karma on Fulcrum for more than a day. He's dangerous, very dangerous."

Unless Lukin was mistaken, the sound of ice tinkling into a glass followed by a long pour was coming from the other end of the line, probably that peaty scotch the major general was so fond of.

"Of course you will have all the equipment you need for the mission, Sasha! When have we ever let you down?" His voice was nonchalant and relaxed, which made Lukin feel like he was in a trap.

"Do you want the short story or should I compose the novel?"

"Don't be difficult, Sasha," Yastrzhembsky's tone turned sharp and sour. "You know how important this is."

Lukin eased off his aggression. "I'm not being difficult, Nikolay. I'm trying to not become a corpse. Send another agent. It will be cheaper."

"We may not have the time. You're already there—this is your assignment." His words were unyielding. "Send us your requisition forms, Sasha. You'll get your equipment. *Proshchay*."

The phone went dead. Lukin tried to convince himself it wasn't indicative of his future in Monaco. *It's always the same,* he thought bleakly. *Old men drinking expensive alcohol in the comfortable chairs of their offices ordering others to risk their lives.*

*****

"She wants us to what?" Moncrief asked incredulously.

"I know it sounds crazy, but they invoked the pact. We don't have much of a choice," Wilson answered.

"Are we sure it's really time magic?" Hobgoblin cast doubt.

"Leader had them reanalyze the formulas just to be sure. One second is a blink of an eye, but in high-frequency trading, it's an eternity. If you could guarantee that no one else has that information for that second—"

"You'd make a killing," Moncrief finished his sentence.

"Whose doing this time magic? Is one of the Lundqvists casting it?" Hobgoblin tried to wrap his head around it.

Wilson shook his head. "I doubt it. I spent all night with Magnus and Karl, and neither of them have a magical bone in their body—they couldn't summon a fart." Moncrief snorted and quieted herself when Wilson looked askance. "Hans has the skill, but not the temperament. He tinkers for the fun of it, just to see what can be done. You should see the random things in his workshop—they are amazing, with no real practical use. It's like watching a Nobel Prize Laureate decide to use all their brain power on memorizing the train tables of the last century."

"But Hans melds technology and magic. Could he have

been tricked by his brothers into concocting some hybrid cable tap?" Moncrief speculated.

Wilson contemplated the notion. "Possibly, but the personal cost to wield that kind of magic is high. And it wouldn't require an attunement circle to work."

"So the working hypothesis is that Ivory Tower's fake Ukrainian blew up the Nemo because someone or something onboard was doing time magic," Moncrief put the pieces together.

Wilson nodded. "It's their protocol. See world-ending magic, blow it up immediately."

Hobgoblin wobbled his head from side to side. "It's not a bad policy."

Moncrief rolled her eyes at Hobgoblin's unabashed affection to the problem-solving abilities of high explosives. "So, where do we go from here?"

Wilson braced himself for Moncrief's reaction. "Hobgoblin and I are staying here and pushing up the timeline. You are going to jaunt around like the carefree heiress that you are supposed to be."

Moncrief gave him a cold stare. "Are you kidding me?"

"No. Making sure Ivory Tower doesn't know you're Salt Mine is imperative. You can always come back afterward or even right before the main event, but you can't be seen as being any part of the process. Not while we are supposed to be working with Lukin," Wilson explained. Moncrief already knew the reasoning was sound; she just didn't like it.

"Or we could just kill Lukin," Hobgoblin suggested.

"You too?" Moncrief called him out. She knew Wilson would like to see him dead. "What is *your* problem with this guy?"

Hobgoblin shrugged. "Dude's a dick."

In that moment, Wilson's esteem for Hobgoblin nudged slightly higher. "I can't believe I'm saying this, but we can't. They evoked the pact, remember?" Moncrief and Hobgoblin stared in disbelief—Wilson was the last person they'd expect to pass on the chance to kill Lukin. "Plus, Leader made me promise."

They both groaned. "I hate it when she does that," Hobgoblin commiserated.

"I still haven't figured out how she does it over the phone," Moncrief puzzled.

"So where do you think they have this time magic stashed?" Hobgoblin returned to the case.

Wilson rubbed the stubble on his jaw. "My gut says it's on Karl's yacht at the marina here. When I went through all the magical security with Hans, he was really excited to talk to someone who could appreciate his work. I get the impression that when it comes to magic, Magnus and Karl are not interested in knowing how the sausage is made as long as they have links by the end of it. But when the *Klymene* came up, Hans got squirrely and very vague."

"In my experience, Hans is always a little squirrely," Moncrief interjected.

"Not when he's talking about magic," Wilson countered.

Moncrief nodded. "Fair point."

"So we're no longer blowing up the boat to flush out the Lundqvists?" Hobgoblin guessed.

"I think it would be unwise until we know what we are dealing with. The last thing we want is to retrieve a piece of time magic from the water only to be pitted against water elementals on steroids," Wilson talked through his logic. "Plus, we have Lukin to consider. We don't know if he knows about you, and if he's in the dark, I don't see a reason to enlighten him." Hobgoblin gave Wilson an approving grin.

Moncrief pouted at their shoptalk, which no longer included her. "I already told Karl I'm leaving Monaco tomorrow, and I have a cousin just outside of Paris I've been meaning to visit. I can be back in Monaco to pick up Westwood in a week's time—do we think the fabric of reality won't break before then?"

Wilson and Hobgoblin sized each other up and threw Lukin into the equation. "Maybe aim for Friday?" Hobgoblin suggested.

Moncrief laughed. "Okay, there will be a pressing matter that requires me to retrieve Westwood sometime on Friday. Let me know if you need me here sooner."

Chapter Twenty-One

Wilson strolled along the shoreline, soaking in the last of the sun's ray after a long day of work. He had spent all day adding magical protections to the upper levels of Lundqvist Investments to complement their other security measures; nothing too difficult, should the Salt Mine ever need to infiltrate, but enough to make it look like he was earning his six-figure fee negotiated yesterday.

Tomorrow was more of the same, and Wednesday he was due to safeguard the house in a similar fashion, but when he brought up visiting the *Klymene*, Karl steered him in a different direction—identifying the man in the video. He would have loved to throw Lukin and the Ivory Tower under the bus, but now that they were working together, Wilson merely eluded to sending out feelers throughout his network. There was always time to implicate them later if he needed to avert suspicion from the Salt Mine.

Wilson didn't press the issue, but the fact that Karl was cagey about him visiting the yacht strengthened his hunch that what he sought was onboard. Wilson needed leverage to get on the Klymene. Fortunately, there was a reason his codename was Fulcrum.

The beach in Larvotto was in transition. The sun worshippers had already left, the nightlife hadn't started yet, and the seaside restaurants were filling up with diners. Wilson stopped by a beachside bar and bought an overpriced bottle of water before taking a seat on the low wall demarcating the businesses from the beach. He was early, but he knew Lukin had been following him since he left the Lundqvist Building. He was content to wait out the clock in the beautiful sunset, replaying the conversation he'd had with Leader in hopes of finding a loophole.

"You will not go after Lukin." She had stated it as fact.

He had mouthed the appropriate response. "Understood. I will not kill Lukin while we are working together under the pact."

"Nor will you set up a trap that will result in his death." She had managed Fulcrum long enough to know his methods.

"I can't guarantee that Lukin won't end up dead by the end of it. We're talking about time magic—things could get messy," he argued.

"I'm serious, Fulcrum. This is more important than your personal vendetta, as justified as you think it is. Next time, it could be us needing help, and if we break the pact, Ivory Tower will not be there to back us up. Do you understand?"

Her words had sliced through him.

He'd relented with a sigh. "Yes, Leader."

"I need to hear you say it, Fulcrum."

Like a chastised child, he'd spoken the litany. "I will not break the pact. I will work with Lukin until the time magic has been neutralized. I will give him twenty-four hours afterward to get away."

"And you have to let him know once the clock has started," she'd added at the last minute.

"And I'll let him know when the clock has started," Wilson had repeated dutifully.

He turned it around in his mind. She hadn't left him much wiggle room, which was how he knew she was serious. But there was always a corner case—a perfect storm where he didn't do anything and Lukin would end up dead. He just had to ferret it out.

Just then, the man who had been following him for the past twenty minutes sat a little less than a meter away: far enough that it didn't look like they were together, but close enough to speak. He was magicked all to hell—the contestants on RuPaul's Drag Race wore fewer layers of glamour—but he tripped Wilson's thread of will as soon as he sat down. There was no doubt in his mind that this was Lukin.

Wilson raised the bottle to his lips and mumbled out the side of his mouth right before he took a swing of water, "Were you followed?"

Lukin took off his left shoe, knocking out the sand inside. "Of course not."

Wilson took his mobile out of his pocket and blended in with the masses who were too busy looking at their phones to notice the beautiful colors in the sky. "We honor the pact," he spoke softly.

"As do we," Lukin replied. He undid the laces before slipping the shoe back on.

"I'm already in," Wilson asserted lead on the operation.

"Does this mean you know the location and form of the threat?" Lukin bent down and tightened the laces.

"I have my suspicions, but I can't get close enough to verify." Wilson held his phone up like he was talking a selfie: #beachlife.

"What do you need?" Lukin started the routine on his right shoe.

"An attack, non-lethal. You've hit their business. I need something personal."

"Location?" Lukin asked as he brushed inside his right shoe with his hand.

"The house. I haven't warded it yet, and those already in place are against supernatural creatures," Wilson answered before taking another gulp of water.

"Time frame?" Lukin slipped his right foot back into his shoe.

"In the next thirty-six hours." Wilson took off his sunglasses and cleaned them on his shirt.

"Consider it done." Lukin tied his laces and left Wilson on the bench sipping water and staring at the sunset.

Wilson dissected the conversation, what was said and unsaid. There was no mention of Hobgoblin, and the Russian readily accepted the task. Did he honestly not know or was he just keeping his cards close to his chest? It was hard to say with Lukin. Either way, things were in motion. All he had to do was play his part until he got the inevitable panicked call from the Lundqvists.

A cool breeze swept off the sea as the streaks of orange, pink, and red in the sky blended with their reflections on the water. The fact that this was an artificial beach and those colors were the byproduct of pollution was not lost on Wilson. Nothing was as it seemed, and even poison had a pretty side. He waited ten more minutes before leaving and sent a message to Hobgoblin: *Boris bound, ETA +/-36.* He tossed his empty water bottle into a recycling bin and made his way back to the red SUV that had become his rental car now that Hobgoblin was lying low.

Chapter Twenty-Two

The Klymene, seventy miles west of Corsica, Mediterranean Sea
28th of August, 02:42 a.m. (GMT+2)

Wilson had to hand it to Lukin—he had asked for personal; the Russian nailed it. It was Magnus that had called Westwood, and his fear had outstripped his considerable indignation—someone had attacked the Lundqvist family home! Wilson had raced to the scene and taken charge of the stunned family, inserting Hobgoblin as his associate in charge of the investigation at the estate while Wilson secured the family's safety.

It had taken little prodding to get everyone aboard the *Klymene*. It was a fully kitted out luxury yacht that Hans had warded, a floating fortress they could sail into the middle of the sea and still maintain communications with the outside world. Most importantly, they could keep up appearances without alerting their investors of their distress. What family in Monaco didn't take time on the sea in August?

Wilson had staged the whole thing so well that by the time they left the marina in Monaco, the Lundqvists had allowed themselves to be soothed by the water. The pair of armed guards Wilson had brought along didn't hurt, either. His position as security specialist had granted Wilson access to all four levels of the yacht and he abused his privilege as soon as possible. A quick walk-through ruled out the spectacular but non-magical treasures Karl had on display, which only left the mysterious door on the lowest level. On first pass, he'd given it a cursory glance—Westwood was there to protect the Lundqvist family and an intruder coming out of a locked and warded door was hardly a threat.

Wilson checked the monitors, ensuring that everyone on board was sleeping except for the two guards who patrolled the main deck. While the guards wouldn't think anything of Wilson going downstairs—his sleeping quarters were below deck—he nevertheless timed his descent from the top deck to the bottom to avoid their detection.

The thick marine carpet of the interior padded his steps as he stealthily approached the thick teak door. An ordinary person would have marveled at the ornate inlay on its surface; however, Wilson knew them to be runes, along with the ones invisible to untrained eyes. Whatever was behind this door, it was warded to the hilt. Hans was a strange one, but the door left no doubt that he knew his stuff when pressed.

Wilson took photos of the runes that were visible to mundane sight and quickly sketched the ones that were only visible to his threaded will. The invisible wards were easy enough to identify—averting the gaze of Poseidon, not that unusual for an ocean-bound vessel—but he was having more problems with the ones on the door. While he didn't recognize them immediately, there was something familiar about them. He had this niggling notion that he had come across them at one time, if only he could remember. He stashed his phone away and crept back to the top deck.

The first thing Wilson did was check the screens. The guards continued their rounds like clockwork, blissfully unaware their boss had ever left the command module. They were part of a real security firm the Salt Mine covertly owned. The Mine owned similar firms around the world, as the need for occasional muscle cropped up in their line of work. *Knowing Leader, they all ran at a profit as well.* When Wilson had met them and told them their assignments, he could tell they'd repressed smiles. Who wouldn't want a job where all you had to do was walk around and look scary on a megayacht on the Mediterranean?

Wilson looked over the pictures he'd taken and considered sending the images to Chloe and Dot for identification, but that would probably mean delaying entry into the room for another day. In any other operation, that might be acceptable, but the longer he kept the Lundqvists sequestered on the *Klymene*, the more risk of complication.

He checked the time and decided instead to flip through the gigs of material he had in his portable library. If he identified the sigils himself and deemed it safe to enter, that would give him time to infiltrate the room tonight and figure out how to take care of whatever was inside.

It took an hour, but Wilson eventually found what he was looking for in the lost chapters of *The Ogdoad and Ennead*. It was an ancient Hermetic document ascribed to Hermes Trismegistus, an Egyptian magus from the second or third century BCE. They were all signs oriented around the life cycle: conception, birth, youth, adulthood, age, and death. The entire spectrum of the human condition was inscribed upon the door, except they were inscribed backwards, which was why he didn't immediately recognize them.

There was only one reason to inscribe symbols backwards: to funnel power in the opposite direction. Wilson had seen this tactic used before on sealed pottery, but not on doors. These runes were put in place to keep something inside, not prevent entry.

With that discovery, he knew what he had to do. He waited until the guards were nearby and audibly stepped down the stairs until he was on the main deck. "Everything's quiet. I'm going to get a few hours of shut eye, but I'll be back to relieve you guys by seven." The guards nodded and resumed their circuit.

He went into his quarters and gathered his esoteric kit. He swapped out his standard European-banishment bullets for a custom load comprised of a mix of European, Middle Eastern, and North African—he didn't know what he was going to encounter behind the door and it never hurt to be prepared. Before he left his room, he paused to listen—nothing but the rocking of the yacht in the sea and the buzz of mechanical systems that constantly ran.

Wilson quietly glided down to the fourth floor, donned his gloves, and pulled out his tools. He checked his watch to time himself before starting. Although it was a solid lock, it wasn't immune to his picks. *Less than two minutes. Not bad.*

He replaced his tools and steadied himself in front of the door, Glock in hand. He summoned his will—*think, think, think*—to temporally anchor himself. He didn't know if there was any real danger beyond, but as he was dealing with time magic, he didn't feel like chancing it. Once he'd finished, he turned the handle.

He only caught a glimpse of what was inside the room: a gleaming trident in a circle. Before he had time to recognize the symbols around the trident, something came on hard and fast, so fast he didn't even have time to shoot, although he was primed and ready to do so. When it hit, his vision first went blank and then he was falling into a kaleidoscope of colors. Shapes twisted and morphed around him. A noodly appendage reached out for him, and for a brief moment, he was part of eternity. Desperate to shut out the entirety of creation, Wilson closed his eyes and poured his will into repeating the anchoring spell he'd just finished. *Think, think, think...*

Surprisingly, it worked and the vertigo left him as quickly as it set in, replaced by the powerful high rush that always hit him after he spent so much so quickly. He opened his eyes and found himself sitting in the command module of the *Klymene*. The figures of the two guards passed through one of the monitors while the others showed the Lundqvists sleeping. A feeling of déjà vu spiked through his high-happy brain. On a hunch he looked at his watch—2:42 a.m. He instantly sobered up.

Shit, he silently cursed. I'm in a time loop.

Chapter Twenty-Three

Outside the Between
Somewhere in Time

Wilson blinked back to his seat at the monitor. Like always, his watch read 2:42, and he had ninety-three minutes and thirty-two seconds before it would start all over again. *Seems like I've been here before*, he sang to himself.

He could honestly say he had never been caught in a time loop before, nor was it something about which there was much research, but he figured there had to be rules to this sort of thing. It was simply a matter of testing, and ironically, Wilson had all the time in the world because he was outside of time.

Each time the loop reset, he still had all his gear on him. He could access everything on the yacht, but whatever he moved or consumed was reset to its original position at 2:42 a.m. Unfortunately, he couldn't carry over objects with him from loop-to-loop. Apparently, creating copies of the same object broke the logic of the place.

All the electronics still worked, but none of them could reach the outside world. The radio on the yacht only got static on the comm, and there were no bars on anyone's mobile. Wilson could still access what was saved on his phone's physical memory. As a bonus, the battery did reset.

He didn't seem to fatigue or get hungry or thirsty, not that it hadn't stopped him from raiding the pantry on the first pass. He could cast magic but he didn't like to, because he didn't know how karma worked outside of time. He'd tried summoning small creatures, but he couldn't get through—not to fae, lesser devils, or ghosts.

Even though he remembered what happened from previous loops, others didn't. For obvious reasons, he didn't want to test if he could die here, but he *could* kill the guards and they would simply reappear at the next round at 2:42 a.m.

After dozens of loops, he believed he'd worked out roughly what had happened—a time elemental had attacked him. It was the only explanation of how he'd briefly ended up in the Between, a legendary place even among practitioners. He would be there still if he hadn't anchored himself beforehand, and it wouldn't have taken long for his consciousness to sublimate into nothing. Human existence didn't make sense without the passage of time. Regretfully, his anchoring spell hadn't been strong enough to send him back to reality. If it had, he would have returned on the deepest level of the *Klymene* and his Girard-Perregaux would have read 4:16 a.m.

Wilson hadn't dared opening the runed door again—he wasn't sure he would survive another encounter with a time elemental. He felt that he'd gotten lucky the first time and he wasn't going to press his luck. Nonetheless, he still remembered what he saw: a trident. He felt it was safe to assume it was magic, and something intensely powerful based on its guardian—there was no way Hans had summoned and bound time to service. Only legendary creatures and legendary casters could do something like that.

Wilson didn't know of any living legendary casters—people such as Merlin, Circe, Simon Magus, etc.—so he settled upon legendary creatures. There were only so many legends that carried a trident: Poseidon or Neptune—depending on whether one's bent was Greek or Roman—Shiva, maybe Hanuman, and the earthly manifestation of the three pure ones, also known as the authority of heaven among religious Daoists. Based on the process of elimination, Wilson put his money on Poseidon, which would also explain the ward on the door.

On this last pass, Wilson had been determined to get answers—after all, everything was going to reset at 4:12 anyway. When openly confronted with sufficient indication that Wilson was not fooling around, the brothers had folded remarkably fast. Karl and Hans had found the trident during one of their treasure hunts, and once Hans told him it was magic, Karl had ideas—even he had heard of Poseidon's trident. He'd confessed to using the power of the trident to stretch time by a single second so he had more of an advantage with his submarine cable taps, which were all guarded by water elementals also summoned by the trident. Based on the look on Han's face, he hadn't known the full scheme, but Magnus had.

Wilson watched the Lundqvists sleep quietly on the monitors, unaware he knew their secret. He was equal parts livid and disgusted; of all the reasons to risk breaking the world, rich people trying to get richer was by far the most asinine. He couldn't say that he was surprised, however. He let himself fume for a while before he shoved down his emotions—he had bigger fish to fry, and his gut was telling him something he didn't want to listen to.

He was in serious trouble. He was far outclassed by the time elemental, and there was no cavalry to call upon. Clover wasn't going to show up in her jet with a suitcase full of magical charms and weapons. Chloe and Dot weren't going to send him the answer. Karl Lundqvist was going to continue to threaten the entire world for more money until someone stopped him. And if Wilson didn't figure a way out of here, he had passed on what would have become his last chance to see Alex, all because it was complicated.

The way he saw it, he had one shot: summon a creature that could travel through time and defeat a time elemental, preferably one that would also not kill him in the process. That was a very small subset on the supernatural Venn diagram and all of the candidates also fell into the category of "the greater of two evils." After some thought, he eventually decided that none of them would be more interested than Poseidon himself.

Summoning classical Greek gods was a surprisingly easy thing to do for one skilled in magic. They were always quick to answer and loved to meddle in even the pettiest of human affairs. However, they were notoriously mercurial with a terrible sense of wrath couched as justice, so much so that humans had quickly abandoned them for inaccessible entities after only a few short millennia.

In many ways, summoning Greek gods was worse than dealing with devils and faerie. Devils always followed the letter of the law and faeries always told the truth, although never the whole truth. A magician dealing with either of those knew from what direction the danger came.

Greek gods weren't nearly as predictable. They could lie, tell the whole truth, or speak anywhere on the spectrum. Worse, they could simply decide to not do what they promised, something which both devils and faeries couldn't do. They were self-realized and therefore not bound by the material that made them. They had no constraints.

Wilson went to the kitchen and collected the items he would need for the ritual—tea lights to engage the eyes, coffee to engage the nose, and salt to engage the tongue. He quickly made his way to the lowest level of the vessel; he'd decided to conduct the ritual in front of the runed door. There was something very oracular about ending it where it started.

The set up was easy compared to summoning devils or fae. Summoning those entities required concentration on crafting the circle and other protections correctly. It required focus on saying the incantation exactly as it should be said. It required a high level of skill and discipline to summon devils, fae, or demons because that was how you protected yourself from them.

Gods were another matter; there was no need for any of that. You couldn't protect yourself from a god. You submitted or died. Only another god could protect a human from a god. Needless to say, Wilson didn't have such a protector nor could he acquire one.

Wilson lit seven tea light candles in a circle large enough to hold himself. He put a bowl of ground coffee down and circled the whole thing in a ring of salt. Last, he summoned his will and marred the invisible sigil on the door—now Poseidon could see his trident.

Wilson got into the saline circle and prostrated himself— his only hope was to take the lowly position of a petitioner. He started singing his chorus; his Greek was not as good as his Latin, but it was comprehensible. While he chanted, the *Klymene* started swaying side-to-side as the waters roughened and the winds blew. Wilson could feel the change in pressure but kept his song going until a booming voice spoke.

"Who summons me to the mortal realm?"

Wilson dared not look up; he had one chance to get this right. "I am but a humble supplicant, O great Poseidon, god of the sea, lord of the earth, tamer of horses. I have found something that belongs to you, but when I tried to liberate it, I was shunted outside of time."

The strong life force considered Wilson's words and quizzed the mortal in front of him. "And what would you have done with such a prize?"

Wilson kept his head down. "Such a thing does not belong in the realm of mortals. We have not the depth and wisdom to wield such power."

There was a moment of quiet before Wilson felt the rumble of Poseidon's laughter. "Your answer pleases me, mortal. I will take what is mine and banish the creature that plagues you."

So far, so good, Wilson thought to himself before going out on a limb. "O great one that shakes the earth and skies, does that mean I will be returned to my own time?"

"Is that what you want, little one?" Wilson felt the god's will probe into him. It felt like a heart attack.

"I have unfinished business and promises to keep," Wilson sputtered honestly, trying to ride out the pain.

"Then so it shall be," Poseidon pronounced as he ripped the runed door open. Wilson dared a glance into the room and saw the time elemental as a shifting collection of multi-sided mathematical solids that also changed shape as did hypercube representations, but he quickly glued his forehead back to the floor. He had read enough myths and parables to know it was never too late to mess up and suffer the wrath of the gods. Just ask Orpheus—old gods were vicious.

With one hand, Poseidon grabbed the time elemental, squeezing it like farfalle, and with the other summoned his trident. The wind picked up in the room, snuffing out the candles, dispersing the salt, and knocking over the bowl of coffee grounds. The god spoke words of power in a tongue Wilson had never heard before.

Then suddenly, the wind stopped. The quiet seemed deafening compared to the roar of just seconds before. Wilson lifted his chest off the ground, and he saw he was still on the lowest level of the *Klymene*. The runed door was wide open, but the trident was gone, as were the salt, coffee, and tea lights. He patted himself down—he was in one piece and all his gear was on him. He looked at his Girard-Perregaux: 4:16 a.m. Wilson grabbed his phone out of his pocket and opened an app—blessed internet!

Wilson rose to his feet and left the door open—there was no avoiding the issue of the missing trident and if he left the scene undisturbed, it would lend credibility to the yarn he was going to spin. The touch of Poseidon left a distinctive mark that Hans should have no problem identifying for his brothers. Instead, he climbed to the control module to assess the situation.

The water was choppy and there was a persistent drizzle with the occasional arc of lightening—the wake of Poseidon's brief presence in the mortal realm. The guards had donned their ponchos but had not abandoned their post. One of the guards called to him on the way up, "Hey boss, I thought you were getting some shut eye?"

"With this weather? I'm better off dozing in the chair,"

Wilson remarked off-handedly. When he sat down at the monitors once more, the time was 4:20 a.m. He pulled out his phone and took care of a few things. First, a large donation through his bank to cover any karmic costs that happened in the time loop. Second, a message to the Salt Mine that the mission was done. Third, a message to Hobgoblin to let Lukin know his twenty-four hours started at exactly 4:16 a.m.

Chapter Twenty-Four

The Klymene, en route to Monaco, Mediterranean Sea
28th of August, 08:30 a.m. (GMT+2)

Wilson heard the stomping and yelling long before Karl Lundqvist made it to the dining area. He burst through the doorway, red-faced with a throbbing vein on the side of his neck. In that moment, Wilson finally saw his resemblance to Magnus, who had been in various states of anger and outrage since he'd met him.

"Where is it, Westwood?!" Karl bellowed, leveraging his height over the seated Wilson. Camille and Hans were shocked at such a display, but Magnus was no stranger to Karl's tantrums.

Wilson buttered his toast and played dumb, "Where's what?"

Karl slammed his fist down on the table. "You know what I'm talking about. The door is wide open and it's gone!"

"Karl," Magnus reprimanded his brother. "Do lower your voice and shut the door. There is no need to air our business to the entire staff."

"Yes, Karl, sit down and have some coffee," Camille encouraged him to calm down. "Whatever is wrong, I'm sure there is a reasonable explanation." Karl grunted and obeyed, taking a seat opposite Wilson and between his brothers.

She smiled and poured the dark brew in a cup for Karl before addressing Wilson. "Mr. Westwood, now that we're all here, can you please explain what is going on and why we are heading back to Monaco?"

Wilson put down his toast and chased it with a sip of coffee. "Gladly, Mrs. Lundqvist. My men in Monaco were able to locate the person who attacked your home yesterday. It was the same man who broke into Lundquist Investments. After some persuasion, we were able to get some answers. He's Ivory Tower, and he was sent to neutralize the use of forbidden magic."

The table went quiet. Wilson saw confusion on Camille's face and disbelief on Han's. Magnus was nobly trying to cover his panic, while Karl was simply stunned—the overconfident are always amazed when they get caught.

"My associate was able to convince him that it would be in his best interest to let me take care of the problem. It was recommended that he get on the first flight back to Russia, and my men graciously gave him a ride to the nearest airport. To that end, late last night, I returned the purloined item at the root of the problem to its rightful owner," Wilson replied.

"I'm its rightful owner. I found it in a wreck; it was attuned to me. It's mine," Karl insisted.

Wilson held Karl's gaze in his own. "Do you think your

laws and definitions matter to a being like Poseidon? Perhaps you would like to ask Prometheus about that? He's generally screaming in agony, but there are a few hours every day before his liver is consumed when he can talk. Maybe he'd spare a word then?"

"But Heracles rescued him," Karl rebutted, dredging up his murky education regarding Greek mythology.

"Heracles had a good ad agency. I assure you the titan is still bound and suffering."

Karl leaned back in his seat, cowed by the thought.

"How did you do it?" Hans asked with genuine curiosity.

"I disabled the ward directed at Poseidon and he came to claim what is his. I did not inform him who had stolen his trident, only that it was found and better off with him. He must have been in a good mood, because he didn't smash the entire ship and there was only a small squall at sea," Wilson spun his yarn—close to the truth without telling the whole of it.

"So that's why it was so choppy last night," Camille commented blithely.

"I could have kept it and not used it," Karl said defensively.

Wilson gave him a look. *Could you, though?* "I'm afraid that might have been an inadequate solution for the Russian interest and could invite more attention in the future," Wilson explained. "If anyone or anything looks, there is nothing to find. I've taken care of the problem. Everyone is still alive. Your business is better protected. And more important, I can report to Ms. Moncrief that the situation is resolved." The mention of Moncrief elicited the humbling Wilson had been looking for.

Magnus cleared his throat. "We're all glad things have come to a peaceable conclusion without further violence, Mr. Westwood. Surely, no one else needs to know the particular details of this escapade."

Wilson caught the gist of his inference—Magnus wasn't above using forbidden magic, but definitely didn't want others to know. He answered in the language Magnus understood. "You can wire the remainder of my fee to the same bank account as the deposit. It was a pleasure doing business with you, Mr. Lundqvist."

Magnus nodded approvingly. Not only was his position recognized, he liked problems that could be bought off. That he understood. "Of course, Mr. Westwood."

"If you'll excuse me, I have to ready some things before we land," Wilson made his apologies as he rose from the table. He could only imagine the infighting that would take place when it was just family.

It had all been arranged—Moncrief should be in transit and would have the jet ready for takeoff from Nice Côte d'Azur. As soon as the *Klymene* docked, Wilson would meet her at the airport and they would both return stateside. Hobgoblin was already on the move to his next assignment. All agents would be out of the area within twenty-four hours of resolution.

Wilson was zipping his duffle bag when a knock fell on his door. He did a sweep of the room and defensively positioned himself. "Come in."

Hans opened the door wide but didn't step inside. "I didn't know what Karl was doing. I wouldn't have helped him if I had known about the time magic."

So Hans investigated the fourth floor and found the traces of time magic, Wilson thought. "I believe you, Hans," Wilson reassured him. Hans breathed a sigh of relief. Even though they had only met a few days ago, Westwood had become the closest thing to a friend he'd had in a long time. He found so few people tolerable, much less companionable. He would hate to think all was lost because of something his brother had done.

Wilson gauged the moment and decided to plant the seed. "You have a talent for the arcane, Hans. If you would like to use it for some greater purpose, call this number." Wilson handed him a blank card with just a phone number on it.

"I'll consider it, Mr. Westwood," Hans said bluntly. He glanced at the card and created a mnemonic to commit it to memory before stuffing it into his pocket. He would destroy it later so no one else would know. It was a secret, and secrets weren't shared.

Chapter Twenty-Five

Pullup Lake, MI, USA
12th of August, 8:00 p.m. (GMT-4)

Wilson stood in front of the door of his rental house in Corktown and listened for a minute. He heard music punctuated with laughter. He took a deep breath and pressed the doorbell. The laughter stopped and the music was turned down. The curtain of the side window shifted, and within seconds, Martinez answered the door. Her hair was pulled back into a ponytail, and she was in a t-shirt and jeans. Her "Latina AF" apron was covered in flour, as were parts of her face.

"Hey! How was your vacation?" she greeted him warmly.

"Fine, but cut short," Wilson answered succinctly. "Can I come in?"

Martinez shrugged and opened the door wide. "Sure, it's your house."

A familiar voice came from the kitchen, "How do I know if the sugar is creamed into the butter?" The sound of Alex's crutches preceded his arrival in the hallway. His hair was shorter than he used to keep it, and he was significantly more tan, but otherwise he looked very much the same. Moncrief was right—life at sea had suited him.

"Hi," he greeted Wilson.

"Hi," Wilson replied.

Martinez closed the door while Wilson and Husnik stood ten feet apart, staring at each other. "I just remembered that I forgot a crucial ingredient for the recipe," she said as she untied the apron strings and dusted herself off. "I'm just going to run to the store. I've got my phone if you guys need me." She grabbed her wallet, keys, and mobile and disappeared out the front door. The purr of her Hellcat and the peel of the tires soon followed.

"She's subtle," Husnik joked.

Wilson let out a short laugh. "It is one of her finer qualities."

"Mind if I take a seat?" Husnik nodded down to his right leg.

"Of course not," Wilson replied and moved to the couch. Husnik swung around the other side, each aware of each other as they moved through the room.

"I wasn't sure you were ever going to talk to me again," Husnik started.

"I wasn't," Wilson admitted. "I had all the time in the world to think during this last mission, however, and changed my mind. I hated that you disappeared on me, but at least I thought you were dead. I'd be a real dick to ghost you when you know full well that I'm alive and just avoiding you."

Husnik smirked. "That's very big of you."

"Not really. Just trying to avoid shitty karma," Wilson

deflected. "So?"

Husnik dug deep. "I'm sorry for bailing. I felt like shit that you were the one that almost died but I was the one that couldn't take it. I told myself it was the nature of the job, but in reality, I was just chicken. I understand if you don't want anything to do with me. I'm pretty sure Leader can post me somewhere where our paths won't cross, if that's what you want."

Wilson took it in and was quiet for a bit before he spoke. "It's not all your fault." Husnik didn't know what he'd expected, but it wasn't that. Wilson continued, "I had already crossed into the land of the dead by the time you reached me in Utashinai. When you pulled me back, a part of me got left behind, and when you saved me, you put part of yourself in its place."

The words came out faster—Wilson had been carrying this truth alone for far too long. "It was a lifeline, this alien piece that hadn't known death. I was sinking and holding on to it with everything I had. I didn't know it at the time, but I was taking too much without anything to give back. It took me months to figure it all out, and by the time I did, you were dead."

Husnik was stunned—David was generally a man of few words, unless it was to educate you on some historical factoid he had just read. "Why are you telling me all this now?" he asked softly; he didn't want to break whatever this was.

"Because you're alive and I thought you should know,"

Wilson answered simply. "If it were me, I would want to know." Wilson shifted on Martinez's oversized couch. "I'd better go. I don't want to be the one blamed if Martinez's baked goods are a bust."

"You don't have to. You could stay for dinner. She always cooks enough to feed a small army, and she'll have no problem putting you to work on the dishes afterward," Husnik extended an olive branch. Even though they were close enough to touch, he didn't feel he had earned the right to encroach on Wilson's space like that. Whatever they once were was gone, but maybe they could be something entirely different, something less damaging to each other.

"That sounds nice, but I'm leaving town for a bit. Leader cut my vacation short and I have something I have to do. Rain check?" Wilson asked. It sounded sincere.

"Sure. It's not like I'm going anywhere for a while." Husnik pointed to his cast as he rose on his crutches and walked Wilson to the door. "Have a safe trip."

"That's the plan," Wilson reflexively quipped before he could stop himself—that was how they used to say goodbye before one of them left for a mission in the old days. Wilson thought it would sting more than it did, but it was only a small ache. He awkwardly put his arms around Husnik, avoiding his crutches. "It was good seeing you, Alex," he spoke in his ear. He broke contact before Husnik could figure out what was happening.

Epilogue

Yakutsk, Russia
3rd of September, 19:07 p.m. (GMT+9)

The tires of the 737 squealed against the tarmac as the plane touched down. Over the wing, Wilson looked out at the less-than-charming Mezhdunarodnyy Airport. Then again, Yakutsk itself was also less than charming. There wasn't much to be done when the land was permafrost the year round. It didn't exactly lend itself to great architecture.

Grabbing his luggage from the carousel, he picked up his rental—a sturdy UAZ Patriot—and immediately drove to his hotel. It had been a very long flight via LAX then Seoul, and finally Yakutsk, and he badly needed sleep. Check in was fast, the room functional, and before tossing himself under the covers, he checked to make sure his luggage hadn't been tampered with. Finally he secured the door with an additional doorstop and fell asleep as soon as he hit the bed.

He woke fourteen hours later, just before ten in the morning, ordered two meals from room service—one for now and one for later—and showered, shaved, and dressed. He'd just finished assembling his Glock 26 when room service arrived. He tipped just enough to let the server know a quick response was appreciated, but not enough to give him any ideas.

He wolfed down the plain and hardy breakfast, re-packed his belongings, and made his way down to his rental SUV. He was still booked for several nights, but he didn't want to leave his luggage any place where it could wander away. He stopped at a gas station and filled up the Patriot as well as a backup five-liter gas can and took the A-331 westward into the wilderness.

Yakutsk was unique in that it was one of the few large cities that was rather difficult to reach by land. Even by Russian standards, the roads weren't the best maintained once you got out of the city. Dodging the ever-present potholes, he made acceptable time before he pulled off on one of the few dirt roads in search of solitude. He chose one that nearly lacked tire marks and had significant grass growing between the ruts. He tooled down the track for a bit more than a quarter mile from the main road before pulling to the side so that traffic, however unlikely, could make its way past his SUV.

Wilson pulled out his phone and typed an e-mail that he hoped would never be sent. Once it was scheduled, he grabbed his luggage, exited and locked the vehicle, and hiked westward into the quiet, ancient forest that didn't end until it reached Yaroslavl nearly three thousand miles away.

He could no longer see his vehicle after a hundred yards and he marched another hundred before he started searching for a small place exposed to the sun—he didn't want to dig in hard earth. It took a while, but he eventually found a fallen tree that had taken down two of its brethren, creating a gap in the canopy. He retrieved his utility trencher from his luggage and dug a six-inch-deep circle just large enough for him and his luggage to sit within.

Once that was done, he forced himself to eat his second meal—one did not enter the Magh Meall hungry. After pushing down the sandwich, Wilson double-checked that he had everything he needed: a handful of red dust from the center of Australia, a pine cone from a giant sequoia, the fangs of an anaconda, the dried heart of a lion, salted fat from the hump of a Bactrian camel, the bill of a penguin, the tusk of a wild boar, and the final thing, a thing that had taken him nearly a decade to acquire, the scale from a charmed fish.

He used a compass to put down four candles at the cardinal directions and sprinkled a line of crumbled shortbread along the interior of the circular trench. He sat down, lit the candles, and waited until his old mechanical travel alarm clock read 11:55. It was a 1950s Bucherer he'd acquired years ago in Switzerland. When the minute hand turned over, he gathered his will and voiced a simple supplicating chant to the fae. When the Bucherer rang twelve, he ended the chant, closed his eyes, and pushed out his will like a string. Over the next hour, he slowly wound his will round and round the circle he sat within, like making a ball of string with himself at its center.

When the Bucherer next sounded, it chimed thirteen and he was in the Magh Meall, the middle lands, the land between the mortal realm and Faerie, as well as many others. The air outside of Yakutsk was already some of the purest in the world, but it took on a supernatural crispness and beauty, letting Wilson know he had arrived in the Magh Meall before he even opened his eyes.

He was within a small clearing no more than thirty yards in diameter in the middle of an endless forest. The meadow flowers were blooming, and nary a patch of snow graced the ground—it was the Summer Epoch in the Magh Meall. Wilson unzipped his jacket and went to work. He wanted to spend as little time as possible in the middle realms.

He stood in the circle and whistled a unique spell. It was based off spells used to call birds to the whistler, but this call was longer, more complex, and required cutting both forearms while casting. After casting, he listened to see if it had had the desired effect.

In the distance, Wilson heard the distinct sound of massive feet moving unerringly toward him. He instinctively went for his Glock, but forced himself to remain still and unarmed. The ground shook with each step as it approached. He turned toward the sound and waited.

At first it was a non-distinct brown shape moving through the canopy. Wilson guessed it was fifteen feet above the ground. When it finally cleared the trees closest to him, he could see it in full. Standing on massive chicken legs, the hut of Baba Yaga had come to his call. The rough pine door of the hut creaked open, and in the darkness beyond, two coal-like eyes bore down upon him.

THE END

The agents of The Salt Mine will return in *Whip Smart*

Printed in Great Britain
by Amazon